The Ghost of Normandy Road

Haunted Minds I

GW01185901

The Ghost of Normandy Road

The First Book of the Haunted Minds Series

□

□

□

□

© 2015-2020

John Hennessy

Praise for *The Ghost of Normandy Road*

"Great book for fans of young adult horror and dark fairy tales. I loved the ending. I never saw that coming, and briefly sat stunned at what I had just read."

- P Mortimer

"The book comes with an ending that you would not even have dreamed. He freaks me out every single time."

- Editorial Review - Read / Watch / Think.

"The Ghost of Normandy Road has a mature style that left the reader caught in a case of cat & mouse moves. If I was 11 to 13 years of age ... I would be frightened to death."

- Editorial Review - D.R. Mitton

"Get ready to be scared out of your wits!"

- Editorial Review - AJ The Ravenous Reader

"John Hennessy has a way with words and a knack to deliver a spine-tingling tale that will have you looking over your shoulder."

- Editorial Review - S.B.

"I bet even die-hard paranormal fans will not guess the ending."

- Editorial Review - R.K.S.

"I had no idea where this story was going to go, but I was so surprised at the ending!"

- Editorial Review - Melissa Reads A Lot Blog

"Will leave you with a lingering fear in your mind even after reading the book."

- Editorial Review - Book Stop Corner

"I adore a good ghost story and this one was a great ghost story with a twist."

- Editorial Review - Booklover Catlady

"The Ghost of Normandy Road should be an award-winning novel because it is well written and riveting. I highly recommend it for adults, as well as young adults. It is the perfect book for anyone who likes scary stories. It has the kind of cliff-hanger ending that will make you want to read the next book."

- Editorial Review – Kristen Van Kampen, Readers Favourite.

*

The Ghost of Normandy Road won the Silver Award for YA Horror in the 2016 Readers Favourite International Book Contest.

*

Original edition first published in the United Kingdom in 2015.
This edition including the factual epilogue, published 2020.

Text copyright © John Hennessy 2015
The right of John Hennessy to be identified as the author of this work is asserted by him.
Original artwork from Depositphotos.
Typography courtesy of Angie Alaya

ISBN-13: 978-1512381269 (CreateSpace-Assigned)
ISBN-10: 1512381268

A CIP Catalogue record for this book is available from the British Library.

All rights reserved.
This book is sold subject to the condition that it shall not, by way of trade of otherwise, be lent, hired out or otherwise circulated in any form of binding or cover other than that in which it is published. No part of this publication may be reproduced, stored in a retrieval system or transmitted in any form or by any means (electronic, mechanical, photocopying, recording or otherwise) without the prior written permission of the author, John Hennessy.

This is a work of fiction. Names, characters, places, incidents, and dialogues are products of the author's imagination or are used fictitiously. Any resemblance to actual people, living or dead, events or locales is entirely coincedental.

Inspiration for *The Ghost of Normandy Road*

We've all felt it – Fear. For some of us, it's an imagined, magnified and unreal state of affairs. For others, we know what we have seen or felt. It could be a perfectly normal situation that we find ourselves in, and yet it seems like every rational and sensible thought has left our head.

Children, with their heightened sense of wide-eyed wonder always see the world differently to adults. In the hustle and bustle of the world, we can forget that we adults were once children too.

For some of us, that means burying the past because our childhood was filled with memories that maybe we would rather forget.

For others, we look back on our childhood days with fondness and a sense of nostalgia.

As I progressed through my early fictional works, the story of Normandy Road, like most stories, nagged at me on a regular basis, begging to be written.

It's not like it is a new story. In many ways, the story you are about to read is thirty years in the making. However, there was a second more compelling reason as to why this story did not happen earlier in my writing career.

You see, some of the events in the book were things that I did actually experience. It's easy for adults to be dismissive, and say that this is the final act of an overactive imagination. But when I first entered the infamous red-brick house on Normandy Road, it was with a sense of wonder of what might be contained within its walls, but also with a sense of fear, because I really was not supposed to be there.

The Ghost of Normandy Road is the eighth fiction book I have had published, with the planning on this story beginning in 2013, and completed in 2015.

To readers of this story:-

Thanks very much for purchasing *The Ghost of Normandy Road*. I hope you enjoy the story, and do let me know, as I love to hear from fellow readers.

Updates on all the author's books can be found at
www.JohnHennessyBooks.com

Prologue

Every time I go to the house on Normandy Road, I think it will be the last. No matter how many times I do this, I find myself shaking uncontrollably. Perhaps it is understandable. I do this to myself, time and again. Because, I want to feel the excitement, the exhilaration, the fear. Okay, I admit it.

I want to see her.

I know she's there. I've been told about her before. Only in ghost stories, they are just stories, they don't mean anything, nor should they, to you or I. When I am not anywhere near that house on Normandy Road, that's all it is. A house. Nothing more, nothing less.

I want to believe in her. I want to believe in the existence of ghosts.

Oh, I know you will think I'm being silly. Your questions? I'm sure you have many. I bet you have the answers to them all as well.

Do the floorboards creak? Of course they do.
Does the door open slowly, making a sound only those on the other side of the grave could possibly make? You bet.
Do the windows rattle? Yeah, for real.

All houses do this, don't they?

Sigh.

Yes they do. Pretty much all of them.

Come on. Rationalise this. Everyone knows why I shake uncontrollably when I go there. It's because she is real. She exists, and she will not rest in her grave. Why? Because she belongs there, belongs in the house on Normandy Road. She's never going to leave, because she can't. But I can. I tease her every time I go, daring her to scare the living daylights out of me.

Sometimes, I can swear she responds to my dare. But no-one will believe me. No-one believes in ghosts, where I live.

Perhaps they don't believe because I have not followed through on the dare, and lived to tell the tale. I hear them say 'you should spend a night in the house then', or they put it in the rules of threes, you know, like saying 'you should go there, three nights in a row. Whatever is in that place, sure won't like that.'

Of course, it's my own fault. I say I will go and stay the three nights, but I never do. I can't, really. I have to be home soon after school, otherwise Mum will be mad.

To understand, you'd really have to see the world through my eyes. That's the problem with convincing people of the truth. They are only ever willing to accept their version of it.

Everything else, is a *lie*.

Act 1
The Witch of Hill Top Green

T***he route from my school to home takes about fifteen*** minutes to walk, maybe ten if I run. On the days that I dare to pass the house on Normandy Road that stands so tall, foreboding, and yes, terrifying to me, I go quicker. Much quicker. On those days, I don't think Jesus himself could catch me.

It's something my mum would term as 'he's got the fear of God put into him.' That would be a pretty accurate way to describe it. My heart would be fast as I would approach it, and even faster as I passed it. As to what happened to my heart as I ran alongside it, maybe, just maybe it stopped beating for a few moments.

I know you won't believe me, and think that it is the overactive imagination of a child. When you're young, you want to be older, right? I'm only ten years old, and I will soon be eleven. I think I might just be growing up, but I know for a fact that the adults think differently when they look at me.

They think I am scared of my own shadow, and well – they're probably right.

I do have a genuine reason for being scared, I really do. I've been nervous for as long as I can remember. Maybe it is a case of genetics, and my parents have passed their fears on to me.

Every time I pass that house on Normandy Road, I refuse to believe my fears are anything to do with genetics. The fear – the one psychiatrists would say is not real or rational, nor one that could hurt me, takes on a life and persona all of its own.

I believe an entity that is the embodiment of all I fear, resides in that house.

Now I *know* I'm being irrational.

At school, we are always trying to scare each other. Sometimes, it's a dare like going into the girls toilets, even though it's five minutes after hometime and only the teachers remain in the school.

Oh, and the caretaker. He's always there.

And the ghost.

Well. We don't know for sure. There's an old story that the girls failed to confirm or deny, but it is said that a girl died after being locked in the toilets one night.

The official record of her death (say the girls) is that she died from a severe anxiety attack from being locked in the toilets. They said she was found with her eyes sewn up, and her tongue had been ripped out to stop her screaming,

The boys that heard this added something to it.

"She was killed by the Ghost of Normandy Road."

Prior to them saying anything, I never believed there was a ghost on Normandy Road. Our school was in the next road, called Bayswater Road.

There was a church beyond it, and a football stadium on the other side of the road that stands to this day.

Normandy Road had tall houses back then, and it's fair to say that adults were sure to be dwarfed by that house on Normandy Road.

It stood alone, you see. Every other house was semidetached or part of a terraced block – all except that one. Why, I did not know, but I was intrigued to find out.

That's what we kids do. We like to look around – if there's a side entry, a dark alleyway, a broken window or an abandoned house, you can bet we want to check it out.

Not for its historical significance, if it had any, and not because we are without any sense of right and wrong. Don't let anyone just say 'oh, they're kids.'

We know what we are doing – we just happen to rely on the foolishness of society to let us off the hook. I know for a fact that there are some children at the school who play the 'I'm only a child, I didn't know it was wrong' card on purpose.

As for me, I probably had one of those faces that looked innocent in one way, only to be ratted out by my *guilty as charged* expression.

Sometimes, it was innocent enough. I would be unable to wait to open at least one Christmas or birthday present. I would sneak down the stairs, placing one foot, then another on the far side of the stairwell.

Life was very simple back then. We had a bit of blue carpet that covered the stairs, except for the edges where I now depended on keeping my balance, my safety and my secret. In fact, falling down the stairs and breaking my neck would have been preferable to my mum or anyone else in the family catching me.

I wasn't supposed to be out of bed. Ten-year-old children were supposed to go to bed early, quietly, and stay there until the right time to get up for school.

Ugh.

School.

School itself was fine. Looking back, it's hard to know exactly what we learned in class. I think we had fun for the most part. There was Miss McManus, who would teach us almost every lesson.

Maths, English, Music, she'd do it all.

Sometimes, we'd get Mrs Oakley, who was a Nazi in a twinset. Okay, I'm being a little unkind. That sort of title was better reserved for Mrs Pearson (or Mizz Pearson, we were never quite sure and she was unlikely to explain her married status, or otherwise, to a class of school children) whose contempt for us was barely concealed.

Mr Flanagan would teach us Maths too, along with Geography.

P.E class would involve having to change with the other schoolchildren, which I disliked intensely. Not for the bizarre communal situation, no, it was just that certain boys would take it upon themselves to talk when they weren't supposed to, and our class would be harder as a result.

"Today, we'll be doing cross-country running."

The teacher was probably going to let us play football, but decided on a change of lesson content just because one boy was sniggering or had been playing another boy up.

Now we would all pay for it.

"Hey," they'd say to me, as we would go for the hated run in the mud, the rain, and the cold, "you had better keep up with the pack. The Witch of Hill Top Green is just behind one of the trees, waiting for you to pass."

I'd fight back with words. "Witches wouldn't hide in trees. They wouldn't have too. And it's you who needs to keep up with the pack, not me. You watch out for the bleedin' witch!"

Ah yes, the Witch of Hill Top Green.

We'd all seen her, though no-one admits to it, at least, not openly.

We would run, and it would be pleasant enough. The September grazed our shoulders gently, unlike the harsh glare of early July. Honestly – two weeks before breaking up for the summer holidays, and they are making us run in blistering heat.

In contrast, I almost found myself enjoying the September run. Then, they'd start their annoying tales again.

"Roy's gone missing," said one of them. "I've lapped you lot twice now, and there's no sign of Roy. She must have got him, her bony fingers must be gutting him out right about now."

I would get a poke in the back when I'd attempt to ignore them, and continue on my run.

"Are you listening? She's out there! Out *here*."

No. I am not listening. I'm running, and will keep running until we get back to the school.

Usually, we would see the teacher over the course of the run. Where was he?

The Witch of Hill Top Green has got him, and Roy. Best be happy she hasn't got you.

Yet.

Oh boy. I just want to get back to the school. Up ahead, the area darkened, and the boys behind me have now disappeared beyond my line of sight.

Or maybe she's got them. Maybe she's coming for you.

Next.

No. The Witch of Hill Top Green was a myth, a legend, but there was more than one of us, myself included, who would have testified at the Old Bailey that we had seen a witch.

But it was not something we were supposed to talk about, so we kept quiet, putting on a brave face when anyone would go missing.

The boys wouldn't let it go, even when people would turn up. If a child who was usually in good health had a day off, then the Witch had got them.

It was a scare story that worked though. One teacher took it too far though, asking one of us to draw the supposed Witch of Hill Top Green onto the blackboard.

One of the boys shook his head at the teacher, and refused the white chalk that was being handed to him.

"No sir, I won't do it. That's how she crossed over into this world. Right now, she's contained in the woods by Hill Top. Let's keep her there, right sir?"

Unfortunately for us, *Sir* wasn't having any of it.

"Danny? You'll do it for us, won't you? You'll draw the witch."

One boy, Joseph, was especially scared of the legend, so much so in fact, that he went from being a confident boy who loved physical exercise, to one who became introverted, unsure of himself, a *sap*.

I stood up on very unsteady legs. I had seen no Witch of Hill Top Green, but I had felt something, some kind of presence. That could have just been the first chill of Winter, saying *Hey, I'll be back soon* even though Summer was yet to officially end.

Back then, six weeks of summer holidays seemed almost too long for us. Now, what we would give for six weeks holiday as adults though, right?

We'd never see such days again. Why did we have to spoil it and scare ourselves?

I knew why. As I looked over at Joseph, his big blue eyes pleaded with me not to draw the Witch.

Of course, I had no idea what she looked like. To each of us, she represented something different, but it was always, *always* frightening.

I decided I would keep the drawing simple. A figure wearing a dress, or cape, with a hood. I'd add stick-like arms for good measure. Best to make her eyes small – if they were large, I swear that Joseph would have been old enough to suffer a heart attack.

That was another scare story. "Joe's old man died the other day whilst out running. They say the Witch of Hill Top Green appeared right in front of him on a summer's day, reached into his chest, and pulled his heart right out. As he gasped for breath, she used her other hand to tear one of his lungs out. As he lay dying, the last image he saw was the Witch holding his heart in one hand, his lung in another.

Then she would *eat* them.

That scared me. I wanted to do a run in the summer holidays and get fit before the return to school. I wasn't the 'fat kid' at school exactly, but chubbier than I would like to admit.

I wouldn't have given an Olympic sprinter much trouble during the school's cross-country run back then either.

I took the chalk off Sir. That was it. I would have to do it now. I hated being the focus of everyone's attention. Yet they were waiting to see what I would draw.

If it resonated with more than one boy, I would perhaps have to concede that the Witch really did exist.

But she did not exist. It was designed to make the boys run faster.

I tried to think back to when I first heard of this so-called legend. Maybe one of the teachers had started the rumour. A P.E. teacher, the name of which now escapes me. I know one thing – he no longer works at the school.

As I scanned the class, a friendly face smiled back.

Rebecca.

Oh, how I loved Rebecca. Red hair, freckles on her cheeks, rosy lips. We kissed a lot in class, and Miss McManus never stopped us, bless her.

Rebecca was perfect. After all, she was seven years old. She was an angel. Boys of my age detested kissing girls, making vomiting sounds at the mere mention of it.

Perhaps I did too sometimes, but not when it came to Rebecca. She gave my life reason, and the school, a level of sanity amongst the twisted thoughts of some of the boys.

She looked at me as if to say *Go on, draw it. It's just a silly story. Then we can go back to doing what we normally do, okay Danny?*

I realised I was blushing, so I turned to face the blackboard. Why did Rebecca have to sit in the centre of the classroom today? Why did Sir ask me, of all people, to draw the damned Witch, a figure I had never seen? Had Joseph's father really had a heart attack and died after seeing the Witch?

I didn't know the answer to *any* of these questions.

I looked back over my shoulder in the direction of Joseph one more time. Everything about his body language was pleading with me not to draw the hateful Witch, but Sir had folded his arms, and was critiquing me through those NHS glasses of his.

He thought we couldn't see the bit of sellotape holding the glasses together, but we could. *We could.* We could always see more than what the adults believed of us. With that empowering thought in mind, I began to draw the outline of the Witch.

* * *

I drew the hood first, because I wouldn't have to draw her eyes, nose and mouth.

Why was this?

Because *she didn't actually have a face*, as far as my hazy recollections went.

Her arms were bony, but had bits of skin attached to them. The legend goes that the more she killed, the more bits of skin attached themselves to her bones.

The hood was brown in colour, but the rest of her garment was a hunter green. Just perfect for hiding in the woods.

No legs. I can't justify drawing them just for completeness sake. She didn't have any legs. She glided, homed in, grabbed you, gutted you, killed you. Your mangled corpse forming part of her grotesque body.

I stood back to observe my creation. It didn't look that scary to me, nor to Sir.

He was about to say, 'You can sit back down now, Danny,' when a trickle of liquid splashing on the floor could be heard, followed by a lot of sniggering.

Joseph had wet himself.

The boys around him erupted into laughter. Some of the girls did too, but most sent scowling and disapproving looks in their direction.

Sir told the boy to excuse himself and get cleaned up.

Joseph ran out of the classroom at such a speed, I doubted that the real Witch of Hill Top Green, if she existed at all, could have caught him.

The image looked cartoonish, at best. But that was my opinion. What others thought, and in particular, what the likes of Joseph thought…well – that was something else entirely.

"That's very interesting, Danny. Now settle down, class. We're all afraid of something."

"I'm not," replied one of the boys with a heightened sense of misplaced confidence. "I'm not scared of the Witch of Hill Top Green, the Tooth Fairy with Blood-Red Wings, nor the Ghost of Normandy Road."

More sniggering from the boys. One of them darted a paper aeroplane in my direction. It hit the back of my neck, and fell to the floor.

That was the first time I had heard someone say there was a ghost that haunted Normandy Road. I didn't have to qualify his statement. I knew there was a ghost, and I knew where it was.

Of course, the Witch of Hill Top Green was an old story. The Tooth Fairy with Blood-Red Wings was a new one on me, but that was all about to be explained.

I'd never sleep with a tooth under my pillow ever again.

Act 2
The Tooth Fairy with Blood-Red Wings

"W***hat kind of teacher would allow a boy to be*** frightened out of his wits to the point that he'd wet himself?" Mum asked.

I found myself in the strange position of defending Sir, not that he had ever deserved my entrenched stance. I felt by drawing the witch, especially in the poor, ham-fisted way that I had done – deliberately, I might add, it would make the Witch much less threatening.

Both Joseph and Sir appeared to have disagreed with me, and now, I was having to deal with my mother too.

"It wasn't like that. Joseph is scared of his own shadow, but he likes to be scared. Those boys are always making up scare stories, and he falls for them, every single time."

"So you don't believe in the Witch of Hill Top Green?" Mum asked innocently. She patted me on the head and gave me ten pence. If this kept up, by the age of twenty I would have amassed a small fortune and a flat head.

That's when I gave her one of the stupid, Joseph-type answers that I would soon regret, because, for all my bluster, I was scared too. I just didn't wet myself at the mention of a ghost, or looking at some drawing.

"No," I replied confidently. "It's just a scare story to make us run faster on cross-country. I heard that one of the teachers passed it onto one of the boys, so that he could spread the rumour, and that would make it sound more real."

Mum boiled the kettle and made a pot of tea. She pulled out a white mug of mine that had a big spider printed on it, then changed it to one that was black with odd sized dots.

"Don't you think it would be a true story, if only one of the teachers told you?"

I was ten, but that didn't mean I was *stupid*.

"Actually, the more I hear from the teachers, the less educated I become."

"Oh dear," laughed Mum. "Not liking school much, are we?"

She then paused. I knew something was coming when she paused like that. It was a device designed to throw me off track. One minute she is giving me the Spanish Inquisition on *Tales They're Not Supposed To Talk About At School*, before hitting me with the scariest thing of all.

The kettle had boiled. She poured the water into the cup, whilst smiling impishly at me. It was one of those things I learned women could do – multitasking. I was a one time, one thing kind of brain, and she knew it. They all did.
Don't probe my thoughts Mum. Please.

"So!" Mum exclaimed, a wide beam breaking out over her face. "Who's *Rebecca*?"

My confidence, such a great companion at times like these, decided this line of questioning was a bit too rich for his taste, and I found the butterflies in my stomach were doing the Can-Can on my insides.

I felt physically sick. How did she know?

"Rebecca? Rebecca – who? Who?"

This was unbearable. I was totally in love with Rebecca and she was the girl I was going to marry and have ten thousand babies with. Rebecca, with her red hair, rosy cheeks, gorgeous mouth, cute body. She never walked into school – she glided, she bounced.

Her whole body language screamed happy, a girl who was totally at ease with herself.

"Well? Do you know who she is and are you going to tell me, or is she another figment of you and the boys' imagination?"

"So *you* don't believe in the Witch of Hill Top Green then!"

My confidence had returned. *Ha! Get out of that one, Mum.*

"Rebecca Delaney. I often chat with her mother, you know."

God. Damn. It. Okay Mum, you win. Well played.

I'd been rumbled. That didn't mean I couldn't act cool.

"She's a girl."

"Well, I'll give you an extra sugar in your tea for observation," she replied. "Apparently she's a girl who has your full attention in class. Not worshipping Miss McManus anymore?"

Mum was mocking me. She knew what she was doing. Parents are professionals at torturing their children after all. She knew everything about me, and some things I didn't know. Her tone was playful, *gentle* even. But it was worse than talking about the Witch of Hill Top Green. I wanted to get her back onto that subject, because when I was home, not running by Hill Top, I was safe from the Witch.

Go back to Hell, you bent-nosed gawbeen, I'd say.

I still liked Miss McManus. She had dark hair, a tanned complexion, a curvaceous figure, even though I was too young to know what curvaceous meant. I played the dumb ten-year old child card once again. Besides, Miss McManus was twenty or thirty years older than me. That didn't stop me worshipping her, it just meant Rebecca was getting a share of the spoils now.

"What's *apparently* mean?"

The answer came rapid-fire, but not the one I was expecting.

"I dread to think what they are teaching you at that school," she said with a shake of the head, and added three, no – five biscuits to the plate next to my tea.

I would have to cut down the biscuits, if not for me, for Rebecca's sake.

"It means that you're not paying attention in class," said Mum, expertly avoiding answering my question directly. "It means that you're scaring other boys in class. It means that you're stuck to Rebecca Delaney's face. *Apparently*."

I went silent, not because I was angry with Mum but because she was right. I never thought about the impact on Joseph or the other boys. I was in agreement with Sir – if I drew the shape of the creature, it would go away.

That's not how some of the boys saw it. By drawing my interpretation of the Witch I had given it legitimacy and now, I had given it a portal in which to escape its confines at Hill Top. Now it could get us anyhow, anytime, and anywhere.

It could get Rebecca.

No, I would not let that happen.

"I wasn't stuck to her face."

"Like I said, *apparently*. Though Mrs Delaney thinks it's rather sweet."

I nodded, like one of those toy dogs with the loose necks that you see in the backs of cars sometimes.

I realised that something the boys said could get me out of jail.

"Apparently, there's something even more scary than The Witch of Hill Top Green," I smarted.

"And what would that be?"

"The Tooth Fairy with Blood-Red Wings."

I was laughing, but Mum wasn't. She slammed her cup down on the table so hard that it cracked, spilling tea over her hands. She cursed lightly, but that's a word I would use later in my life. When teachers would say *Where did you learn such bad words like that,* we would say "Home!" and at home, when we were asked the same question, we would say "School!"

I would laugh when I would say that, because it was good to play Mum against the School, and vice versa.

I was not laughing now. She turned around to me and gripped me hard by the shoulders.

"Now you listen to me. There's nothing like that in this world or the next, do you hear me?"

"I hear you. Mum, you're hurting me."

She was. Her nails were digging deep into my shoulders.

"You boys don't know what you're messing with. All this talk about witches and evil tooth.....things. Where will it end?"

She seemed genuinely upset, and had forgotten all about Rebecca too.

I bravely decided to reintroduce her into the conversation.

"She's my girlfriend."

Mum was cleaning up the tea, and gesturing to me to move out of the way, safe from the broken shards of cup that now lay partly on the floor and on the kitchen worksurface.

I had never said the G word before then, and it seemed unfair not to have let Rebecca in on the conversation. Yes, we had chatted a little, but honestly, what do girls and boys have to talk about.

So we stuck to each other's faces.

Mum had regained some of her composure, when the shrill of the telephone threatened to take it away from her again. She grabbed it with such force that the receiver almost fell out of her hand.

"Hello? Oh, hello, hi Rosemary."

Rosemary? That had to be Mrs Delaney. Was she psychic or something?

"No, no, I'm fine. Yes, I heard about that? Oh, did she? How cute!"

It was so annoying listening in on one side of a conversation. Mum agreed, and pointed upstairs to my bedroom. I grabbed my cup, saw that not much of my tea was remaining, and slunk upstairs with thoughts of Rebecca filling my head.

* * *

The thing was, I had always been frightened of Normandy Road. There wasn't anything rational about my thought process, it was just the way I felt.

All the houses on the road looked normal apart from that big red one, and to get to Rebecca, I had to cross over that road, by the house, and head to her modest house in Earlsbury Gardens.

The area had gone down even in the short eleven months I had known Rebecca and it was then that my Mum hit me with it.

Thankfully, she had knocked on the door, and brought me yet another cup of tea. Who needs sleep, anyway?

"Well it seems like your girlfriend will be moving closer to you. Won't that make you happy?"

"Rebecca?"

"Yes, unless you've got any other girls you haven't told me about. How will Miss McManus ever get over you?"

She was smiling again. I didn't want to bring up the whole Tooth Fairy with Blood-Red Wings again, but at least I knew I had one weapon with which to frighten her. Oh, I wasn't an evil child, we had enough of those future jail tenants in our area. But it was good just to have one thing, just *one* thing over her.

"I believe Miss will be just fine. Where's Rebecca moving to?"

"Normandy Road."

It was my turn to drop the cup.

* * *

I don't remember leaving the house, and making a beeline for Rebecca's home on Earlsbury Gardens.

I also don't remember clearing the bed, the stairs, the front door as my feet never touched the ground. How about that for witchcraft?

This couldn't be true. Rebecca could not move into that road. She just couldn't!

I slowed down as I reached Earlsbury Gardens. Children like me rarely take note of the things that they should, like house numbers. On Earlsbury Gardens, the houses were all of a Victorian design. They all looked the same. If only Normandy Road was like that.

I didn't know what I would do when I got to Rebecca's house. What I am I supposed to do? Shout in the middle of the road? I can't knock on the door, that's when Mrs Delaney – or worse, *Mr Delaney* would answer.

They would refuse to let me see Rebecca, then move to Cornwall so that I could never see her again.

I looked up at the window. I wished with all my heart that Rebecca would come to the window. I waited and waited, but had no such luck.

I paced up and down the road. This wasn't a good idea. Earlsbury Gardens looked nice enough, but it had trees on either side of the road, making it look darker than it really should be for that time of year.

I was about to turn away, when a voice whispered my name.

"We'll get in trouble if we're caught," she said, as she grabbed my hand, and the best kind of electricity passed through my body.

I wouldn't mind getting into trouble with Rebecca. In fact, I wanted it to happen. After all, things are always more fun if you don't have permission.

"It's okay, I told my mum I was going over to Jennifer's. What did you tell your mum?"

"I didn't say anything to my mum. I just ran out of there."

We walked around the corner from Earlsbury Gardens, and turned into the road where our school was – Bayswater Road. We climbed over the wall, which you could do back in those days, and made our way to the school playground.

We were kids, all innocent back then. We didn't know anything about anything really, even less about nothing; and in the case of each other, we didn't need to know anything else. We just loved being with each other. Rebecca was my first true love. My only love. I forgot all about being frightened when I was with her.

"I'll have to go back soon," she said. "Do you want to see the new house, so you know where to come next time you feel frightened?"

"I wasn't frightened," I lied.

"Must have been *me* that made you blush then," she smiled. "Come on, it's only down here."

We stopped – that is to say; *I* stopped Rebecca from going any further.

"Why? Why do they do this? Your parents don't have to move, and even if they did, this is the worst possible road to come to."

Rebecca wore a bemused look on her face. Her eyes narrowed a little, but were still huge. I was with her, that's what I should have been concentrating on, but no – I was worried about something that was probably nothing, and living somewhere, or probably nowhere along Normandy Road.

"Dad says we have to move. There's damp in that house, and it's *spreading*."

I would take *damp* any day of the week compared to what resided in Normandy Road.

"Did you tell him? You told him what the boys say, didn't you? That something evil is on that road."

Rebecca laughed.

"Oh come on, Danny! You didn't fall for that old tale, did you? It's just a wind-up. You know, like the Witch of Hill Top Green, and The Tooth Fairy with Blood-Red Wings."

I didn't want to disagree with Rebecca. We were having a good time, and I didn't want to spoil it. Besides, she could tell me that the angels in heaven were the bad guys, and that Lucifer had been given a raw deal, and I would have believed her.

I was happy to agree with Rebecca, that the Tooth Fairy – that particular one, did not exist. I found out about the other Tooth Fairy by accident, but that was okay, all part of growing up.

The way Mum had acted, I believed in the Blood-Red Winged variety – *that* was real. I was dreading the next time I would have a tooth fall out, because, according to one of the boys at school:-

'She wakes you up in the middle of the night, jams her wand into your mouth, splashing blood on your pillow. That's why Sir doesn't smile – she's already got to him. He lost a whole row of teeth. She is what the parents fear, and they'll pass that fear onto us. There's nothing scarier than the demons that won't stay on the locked side of the door.'

So far, so good. I had not seen the blasted Tooth Fairy with Blood-Red Wings, and I could live all of my life and not care if I did.

'It's not the teeth she wants, exactly. It's the blood. Children's blood. It's young, fresh and virginal. Her wand is made from the bones of children who rotted into a pile of flesh, tissue, blood and bone because they got scared.'

Unlike some children I knew, including myself, Rebecca was actually looking forward to moving home, even if it wasn't so far away. Maybe that was the reason for her sunny disposition, because it meant she would still be at the same school, with the same friends and of course, she would know the area. My mood brightened a little.

Bayswater Road, where our school stood winded down and around. My steps slowed as we approached Normandy Road, which forked off to our right.

Rebecca was almost at a skipping pace, her small hand wrapped around mine. She didn't have a care in the world. When I was with her, I was pretty sure that I should not have a care in the world either, but with all my heart, I did not want her to move into this road. I didn't want her anywhere near that house.

In truth, the route home didn't require me to go down Normandy Road at all, it just happened to be the quickest route. I never knew why I was so scared of it, but on reflection, it had to be because the boys' stories had gotten to me. Girls didn't seem to share the same need to scare each other.

Boys are such little bastards, aren't they?

If Rebecca wasn't scared, why was I?

We turned into the road, staying on the same side as the big red house with windows that stared at you like eyes, and a door that would swing open any moment and devour you, like that scene in Texas Chainsaw Massacre.

I did not want that to happen to us. I did not want to be on a butcher's table, looking up to the ceiling as the killer jammed Rebecca's body onto a meat hook, spinning it around for me to see, whilst she gasped her last breaths.

Let's cross over the road, Rebecca. We can do that, can't we?

That was also a stupid idea, because the old house looked even larger when standing on the far side of the road. No, we'll stay on this side. It'll only take a few moments to pass it.

I asked Rebecca the question I had been dreading to ask.

"It's not the old red house, is it?"

Rebecca looked so funny at me. I heard it too – was that really my voice? I thought I sounded like a girl, whilst at the same time knowing Rebecca didn't sound like that. It was some kind of high-pitched tone I wasn't used to. I cleared my throat and repeated the question.

She squeezed my hand even tighter. I was losing blood circulation in my arm, but I was with Rebecca, so such things didn't matter.

"No, of course not," she said. "That house is 110. We are at 116. It's a ruin, anyway. No-one lives there. Do you want to check it out?"

Not unless you're done with life, Rebecca.

"Well, ours is 116. Have you got that? You won't be standing outside looking for me this time, will you?"

No, I could remember the number, that was okay. In addition, there were fewer trees on this road than Earlsbury Gardens. If all came to all, I could just count. 110, 112, 114, 116.

If only Rebecca lived at 118 – no, that was too close. 122, 124 or something like that; then I could see her without having to pass that house.

We walked on, and Rebecca was right, it wasn't far from the school at all. I just wondered how she would cope at night, and selfishly, how would I cope if I wanted to see her at night? The light falls so quickly in October. You're lucky if there is any brightness in the sky after four o'clock.

If a chill passed over me when we approached 110, I failed to notice it until we were beyond the hated place.

It must have been a similar feeling to an agoraphobic who manages to leave their house, and walk up and down the road they've lived on for fifty years, only to discover that nothing could or would actually happen to them. The irrational fear caused physical reactions that were real, but the fear itself was unreal. They would pass, and so would I.

I breathed a huge sigh of relief. Rebecca was so cool, she kept hold of my hand the whole time. The whole time, that is, that I was being a wuss.

I kissed her without even thinking about it. She kissed me back, but had one eye towards her home, even though she knew her parents were not in it yet. We had never kissed in public, not like that before, and I think it shocked the normally unflappable Rebecca as much as my impulsiveness shocked me.

I was just caught up in the moment. I didn't think the house held any power over me, or any of us, when I was with Rebecca. I just couldn't seem to deal with it when I wasn't with her.

The agoraphobic would say, 'Ah yes, I know what you mean. I feel the same. I can't leave the house on my own. I have to be with someone. Someone I can trust."

I certainly trusted Rebecca, but this was my first feeling of love. I was a young child, and I suppose, defining love was difficult. But with Rebecca, even if all the evils in the world didn't melt away, they became manageable somehow.

I don't know what I would do, or how I would manage, if anything happened to her.

Her house looked....well, it looked like every other house on Normandy Road. Every other house but one, and I knew which one that was.

A small garden at the front, a big front window on the ground floor, two windows on top.

"There's a room you can't see," said Rebecca, "but it will be an extra room for me. Dad's going to convert the attic, and when he does, you can come up there and stay with me. It'll be fun!"

I'm sure Mr and Mrs Delaney would have something to say that would crush Rebecca's view of the world, but I would let that slide for now.

Something didn't feel right. I felt a little light-headed. I didn't want Rebecca to see me in anything other than a good light, but I would learn as I age that maybe, you just had to learn to be comfortable in your own skin, so that you could be a light in the company of others.

The house, though bolted on to the next building, did have a narrow passageway at the side. Rebecca opened the door, explaining how her father was yet to put a lock on it from the inside, but had pushed a wheelie bin up next to it in the meantime. *Makeshift security*, her mother had called it. Her father gave several assurances that he would get the door securely locked.

"But for now, we can go inside," sang Rebecca's voice.

She kicked the door shut.

"We're alone," she giggled.

Throwing her arms around me, we kissed again, and while I was enjoying it, that lightheaded feeling had returned. Something was wet, and it wasn't just Rebecca's mouth.

I was bleeding.

"Oh! Oh, goodness!" exclaimed Rebecca, who reached for her dress pocket and produced a napkin, and instead of being repulsed, started to clean my face up. She was such a sweet girl.

"You're having a nosebleed! Pinch your nose, that's how you stop it, and tilt your head back too."

Is there anything Rebecca didn't know? After a few moments, I started to feel better. I really didn't know what had happened. I have never had a nosebleed before.

"That's better," she said, looking pleased with herself. I must have had a strained and embarrassed look on myself, because she added, "Hey, it's fine. Let's get back to what we were doing!"

It was nice, very nice, to be with Rebecca. She was fun, cool, pretty and smart. Everything I like about a girl. Her mouth tasted good, like strawberries.

We must have been kissing for longer than any of Miss McManus' classes, because our mouths started to hurt, but it was more than that. Now, something was affecting Rebecca.

"Oh, oh that's horrible," she said, releasing herself from my grip.

At first, I thought I had done something wrong. She looked around in her dress pocket again, found another amount of material – a cotton ball, this time, and coughed something up.

"Are you alright, Rebecca? What's wrong?"

She sighed heavily, and put whatever the object was, into her hand, wrapped the cotton ball around it, and looked at me with those huge blue eyes of hers.

"I'm going to tell you something I've never told anyone before. Then I'm going to ask you something, and swear you to secrecy. Third, if something happens to me, I want you to know, it's not your fault."

I looked at Rebecca with confusion and bewilderment on my face. I started to speak, but she mouthed *Not Here.*

She ushered me out of the side entry. "It's dark. How fast can you run?"

"Fast, but not as fast as I'd like."

"It'll have to do." She handed the object in the cotton wool ball to me, instructed me to put it away, and not look at it until she told me to.

We both made a run for it. Back up Normandy Road, around to Bayswater Road, into Earlsbury Gardens. A five minute run if we were quick, a three minute run if we were really quick.

If the Ghost of Normandy Road, The Tooth Fairy with Blood Red Wings or The Witch of Hill Top Green decided to show up at that moment, I bet I could make it to Rebecca's current home in about three seconds.

For her part, Rebecca had let go of my hand and started her run without me. Whilst she had a good head start, I knew I could catch up with her. I wasn't about to be beaten by a girl, even if that girl was Rebecca.

Normandy Road rises before turning into Bayswater Road, which in turn rises again, before flattening at out the Gardens. Rebecca was literally flying up the road, her red shoes and white dress with cherries blurring everything in front of me.

"Reb-," I called, but she was too fast. Far too fast. "Rebecca! Will you slow down. Slow-"

No. I did not want that bloody head rush again. Whatever had spooked Rebecca, she wouldn't tell me until we got to the top of the road.

I gave chase as hard as I could, but I knew that this was the day a girl beat me in a race. If any boys from school were watching, and they could quite possibly live in Normandy Road, they would watch, and laugh, and tell everyone at school the next day.

Rebecca had disappeared around the corner into Bayswater Road. Why had she left me with the dust flying into the air from her trainers? She knew how I felt about this road. I know my fear was irrational, and I have been up and down the road more times than I can possibly count.

"Rebecca!" Not for the first time that day, my voice was strange – no, make that *strained*. If Rebecca could hear me, she wasn't turning back. She had gone.

When I made it to Bayswater Road, I fully expected to see Rebecca. But I didn't. She was nowhere to be seen. She couldn't have kept that speed up, surely?

I slowed to a sluggish pace, which turned into an even more sluggish walk. She had given me something, not a keepsake, not something to share between sweethearts, and I wanted so bad to check and see what it was. But I wouldn't do that to her. Still, I couldn't help but feel a bit miffed that she had just fled, leaving me behind.

Finally, just beyond our school at Bayswater Road, I could see her. She wasn't facing me, in fact, she was looking away in the distance at something, though what she was looking at, I could only guess.

I placed a hand on her shoulder and she made me jump, as she jumped.

"Reb! What's up? I thought I was the nervous one."

She turned and looked at me, her eyes portrayed a sorrowful glare.

"First, you were bleeding, then I was bleeding. I don't know if it's the place that is the problem, or if you are the problem, or something else. I just don't know. That's why I ran as fast as I did."

If *I* was the problem? Whatever did she mean?

"Rebecca, you're scaring me with this kind of talk."

"So tell me, do you ever bleed like that?"

I shook my head. I never had a nosebleed before, and I never wanted one again.

"I tasted blood in my mouth. Now, I have to go, my parents will be looking for me. Let me give you this-"

Rebecca produced a pen and paper from the small bag she kept around her waist. It never failed to surprise me just how resourceful she was. She began to scribble furiously, and as she wrote, I could see goosebumps appear on her arms. It was late in the year, and Rebecca was rarely seen with a coat. Sometimes, she would wear a cardigan that would barely cover her back, but not today, and not for many days had she dressed like that. I didn't notice the way other girls dressed, only her. She filled my thoughts, all of the time, and it scared me to know that she was scared.

She pressed the note into my hand, and pleaded with me not to read it until I was home, and preparing for sleep. I looked at her with a *what the hell* expression, and could only look on with further confusion as she knocked on her home door and waited.

When she wasn't answered straight away, she turned to me and waved her hand, partly saying *goodbye* and the other meaning was *get out of here now.*

Okay Rebecca, I know when I'm not wanted.

I could understand. My family wouldn't want me bringing round girlfriends either. In any case, my brother and sisters would take it in turns to tease me, before ganging up on me. I wouldn't let them know anything personal about me. It's best to keep your guard up, because once your defence is down, people can and will stamp all over you.

I felt that Rebecca was different, so if she wanted me to go, there had to be a good reason. I headed home, but diverted the long way down Earlsbury Gardens, and through to Canterbury Road. By doing that, you could bypass Normandy Road altogether. But I couldn't get my mother, sister or Rebecca to understand that.

There were a group of older boys on Canterbury Road. They weren't doing anything – at least, that's what they would tell the police.

I reckoned they were about fifteen or sixteen years old, and there were four of them. Just one would be more than a match for me. I considered retreating back, and facing Normandy Road on my own.

I wondered which death would be worse. Beaten by fists I could see, or torn apart by hands that I couldn't?

If I ran, the boys would definitely look in my direction, and potentially give chase. There would be no way to outrun them. They would check my pockets, take that precious handwritten note from Rebecca, and the object she gave me.

I felt for a reassuring bump in my back pocket. It was still there.

Just then, one of the boys looked up. The game was over.

"Hey!" he shouted. "Hey you!"

The others started to laugh. I expect a pack of wolves would act like this against a wounded bison. I did not want to play the part of the bison, so I began my run. As much as I was scared of what was, or what was *not* on Normandy Road, these boys were not a figment of my imagination. They were real, and they could hurt me.

I decided to retreat, because from where I was currently standing, it had a downward slope, rather steep in fact. So yes, I was scared, but maybe this was a test for me; a coming of age type of thing. It was like slaying two demons with one stone, as it were.

While I was processing all of this information, my legs were already moving faster than I have ever run.

It wasn't long before my short legs had reached the red house on Normandy Road. As I ran alongside it, I thought one of the huge chimney pots would launch itself off the roof and land on me, crushing every single bone in my body.

How the mind plays tricks on us, yet so many of us are caught in its power.

I knew I shouldn't, but I looked up at one of the windows.

Someone, or *something*, was looking back at me.

I stopped running, even though every single rational thought that remained in my head told me to keep going.

How do you distinguish rational thoughts from the voices in your head? Moreover, how does a ten-year-old do that?

The front door to the big house wasn't secure. The door barely hung on its hinges, and the garden would have been a work of wonder at one time, but was now overgrown with weeds. A path both to and through the house had been worn down by a combination of boys on bicycles, cats on the prowl or hunting for shelter, and maybe people too. *Squatters*, I think my mum called them.

This was Autumn, and the figure staring at me from the window appeared to be wearing some kind of flimsy nightdress or shirt. She looked human for the most part, her hair greyed and thinning at the temples, her skin bore a strained, gaunt look, and her arms were bony and disfigured by blue veins.

I couldn't take my eyes off her. I tried to process where I had seen her before; because she did seem familiar to me. But she could not be a real, living human.

She placed her hand on the window and her palm started to darken. I could then see she was bleeding. I wanted to run, run anywhere, even into that house where she resided. The boys' shouts were getting louder and by now, I would have lost any advantage I had had over them.

Her neck turned her face towards me, and it was turned blue with the veins that protruded from her throat.

She removed her bleeding hand from the window, and trails of blood eased their way down. With her hand she beckoned towards me, and I found myself, inexplicably making me way through the undergrowth, before I had crossed into the actual house itself.

Inside, it was difficult to describe the images in front of me. I felt like the air was pushing me down towards the floor. The boys 'shouts had gotten louder, but less clear. I knew they were close, *very* close, but there was a blanket of energy in the house that was pressing me close to the floor. I lay down on the cold concrete. Bits of old carpet cushioned my small body.

Closing the hands over my eyes, I waited for either the shape at the window, the boys who followed me, or fear itself to claim me.

* * *

The boys were in the hallway. There was a staircase, right in the center of the main room. They looked around, and were mindful of a chandelier above them that was loosened from its base, and looked like it had waited a long time for some fool to enter, and crash down on them, keeping them in the old house forever.

Thoughts of Rebecca were keeping me alive. It was good thought, a pleasant and happy one. The boys were of a different mindset. They were calling for me, saying what they were going to do to me once they got a hold of me. Something about smashing my face in, having a stamp party on my stomach. None of which sounded pleasant at all.

I could see them, but for the life of me, I could not understand why they could not see *me*.

"Where are you, you little brat?" one of them said.

"We're going to beat you so hard for running from us," added a second.

"You are *never* going home again," the third boy added menacingly. He sounded like he meant it.

The next moment, I could see the figure on the stairs. The boys looked at her too, and had they viewed what I did earlier at the window, they would have come to the same conclusion that I had.

This is not a human.

They could see her. They looked at her, and laughed.

"Well, someone's lost. Forgot how to dress today?"

Her expression, that of stone, did not change, she just remained on the third step from the bottom of the stairs. I could see her bare feet, most of the nails had been torn off. There was a bruise the size of an orange on her right leg.

"We're looking for someone. Someone who ran in here. Have you seen him?"

She declined to answer with words. Instead, she lifted her hand, which by now they could see was old and decayed. One by one, she pointed to them.

"Bit late for Eeny Meeny Miny Mo, isn't it?" laughed one of them.

Finally she turned to me. Whatever had been pressing me down, had lifted. I felt I could stand and actually have the power to make my legs obey me.

The boys remained rooted to the spot. I looked back at the girl, wanting her to do something – something crazy, like leave the house with me, but leave the boys there. She shook her head.

I found myself outside. By now, it was raining, and the door that had hung precariously on its hinges, appeared to have undergone some form of regeneration.

There was nothing for it, but to get along home. As I walked towards my house, I was sure I could hear the sounds of three boys screaming, as something smashed their face, crushed their neck, and stamped all over their bodies.

* * *

I ran home at a speed that would have almost seen me come in first place – if we'd been doing cross-country running, that is.

My parents were at home, and my mum shouted something about not getting mud marks on the floor. She obviously thought that was more important to remark on, than the distressed state I was in.

Typical parents.

As I jumped the stairs three at a time, I heard them both mumbling something about *typical kids*. In my bedroom, I collapsed stomach-first onto the very welcoming bed, and reached into my back pocket.

I wondered what Rebecca had been up to. I believed the heavy bleeding we had both experienced was caused by that house. Something wanted to harm us, that was for sure, yet I had been allowed to leave, whilst what happened to those boys was just unimaginable.

I rolled onto my back, and planned to open the object Rebecca had pressed into my hand. I thought it would be like a girlish keepsake – a hairpin of hers, perhaps, or one of those two pence rings you could get from the chewing gum machines.

I pressed my fingers around the cotton ball until a more defined shape appeared. It was too small to be a hairpin. Also, it felt hard and blunt.

Could it be a magic stone or something?

Annoyed with myself for having stupid yet fantastical ideas, I gently unwrapped the cotton wool, freeing the object.

I gasped as it fell onto my stomach. It was a tooth.

* * *

It would be quite fair to say that if Rebecca gave me anything, and I do mean anything, I would have kept it in my possession unless she wanted it back, and I would have killed anyone who would have dared to take it.

But a tooth that had detached itself from her mouth would have almost certainly been last on my guess list. I wasn't as repulsed at it as I thought I would. I had lost teeth before; it was all part of growing up, Mum says.

She would always tell me to put it under the pillow, so that the Tooth Fairy would come. There was always a payment for that tooth – most times, for normal sized teeth, I would get twenty pence, other teeth, like a molar, could get me somewhere near a pound.

If only I had more teeth to loosen from my mouth, I could have made a small fortune.

Rebecca had a cute mouth, and barring the one I held in my hand, a perfect set of teeth. I thought it was kind of a gruesome keepsake, and that's what troubled me. Rebecca didn't like gruesome things. In fact, I was sure she would have preferred to have the tooth fall to the ground, rather than to have her touch it.

I wasn't repulsed by it. In fact, I thought it was rather sweet. After all, once they're out, such things don't go back into your body.

It was unusual keepsake, but a keepsake nonetheless, and although the tooth was huge, it would not be going under the pillow. Besides, I could get five pounds for this. I would have had to bargain with the Tooth Fairy though.

A combination of the rain and the day's events worked to send me to sleep. If anyone had been watching me, they would have called for the men in white coats. I tossed and turned on the bed, almost violent in a way. Many times I would kick out at some unseen force. My overactive imagination was at work once again.

* * *

I woke with a start. The house seemed quiet, and that meant one of two things – either my parents were asleep, or they were both out. I checked my watch. Through blurry eyes I could make out what the digital screen said. My father swore that a proper clockface could not be beaten, that you always knew the time of day, and the design ensured that even in the dark, the reflection of the face would display the correct time. He had other sayings too, such as *if you don't know the time of day, you don't know anything.*

He detested modern, digital timepieces and especially those that had a backlight for a watch. One time, I had called him *old* which didn't go down too well.

The time was 2:04am. Had I been asleep that long?

Where was the tooth? The precious one Rebecca had given me?

So, my parents were both asleep. Good. I didn't like to be alone now, even though I had begged for my own room for as long as I could remember.

I didn't want to put the light on, because I had done that before in the night, and Mum complained that it had woken her up. The backlight on my watch was a poor substitute.

I could not find the tooth.

A curse, one my father sometimes used, escaped from me before I knew it. I immediately apologised to God, even though he's the one who is supposed to have given us free will.

I eased myself up into a sitting position. My head and upper body were fine, if perspiring a little. Something else was wrong. My legs felt clammy, and paper-like. That's a strange way to describe it, but I felt if I were to swing my legs out of the bed, and attempt to stand on them, I would crash to the floor – simple as that.

I felt under the bed for the shape of my legs. Worryingly, the clammy, paper-like feeling increased.

Then the word came to me.

My legs felt like *seaweed.*

There was a strange smell in the room, and I did not like it at all. I checked my watch again; which must have malfunctioned because the time of 2:04 am remained on-screen.

I wasn't aware seaweed had a smell. It was rather like the smell of Bonfire Night, which I didn't like to go to, but I wouldn't mind watching from my bedroom window.

Maybe I was affected by too many adverts on the television, but someone was always getting burned by those sparklers. Mum would exclaim incredulously *'Why do they let children hold explosives in their hands,'* whereas my father would be saying something to the contrary, usually meant to annoy her.

'It's just a bit of fun,' he'd say.

The Tooth Fairy was supposed to be a bit of fun too. In class one time, we were asked to draw an event from the day before.

I had just lost tooth number three, and yet I was a whole one pound and fifty pence to the good, so I was happy.

A fair trade in 1980's money. I wonder what they are giving the kids now?

Me and Rebecca may have kissed long before that day, but I do recall it was the first thing I remember asking her. I didn't have the right colours for my project, and I had a reasonable flair for art.

I drew the outline in pencil, that's how I did it back then. After the basic structure was there, I would shape it, add density and layers, and work in the colours.

In my head, the drawings looked awesome. In reality, they never looked quite as good.

"Are you finished with that crayon, Rebecca?" I asked.

"Which one?" Even back then, she always wore a smile on her face. "I've got loads."

I grabbed two, a pink crayon, and a light grey one. The wings of the Tooth Fairy were ivory, but light grey would have to do.

When I had finished, there were many *oohs* and *ahhs* in class, even from the boys.

"Well, this is marvellous," said Miss McManus. "I really like how you've draw this, with the fairy pointing her wand towards houses in the street. The blue hue of the night sky, you really made it look so magical. On a more serious note, please – none of you are to start ripping your teeth out. There's other ways to get some money."

"What rubbish," said one boy. "My drawing was of the real Tooth Fairy – the one with Blood-Red Wings, not something out of Disney."

He held up his drawing in protest.

"Darren, I think that's-"

"DISGUSTING!" screamed one of the girls. For her own part, Rebecca said nothing, simply choosing to avert her eyes. "Miss – please, take it and throw it away!"

The image was certainly disturbing, but I had to admit, it was a braver choice than mine. I had played it safe. If I always played it this safe in life, and took no risks at all, I would achieve nothing – not now, not ever.

"Beats your Tooth Fairy to Hell, doesn't it?" Darren said to me. "You know why? Because mine is *from* Hell."

His drawing was not of a playful, magical entity. Where mine had cute eyes, his was drawn with slits. Where my drawing had big wings with an ethereal outline, his was hellish – the wings were a black and red mosaic of all that was gruesome in the world.

Then I could see what he had drawn on top of the wings. At first, they looked like lumps. They were actually teeth – the single teeth of children that the Tooth Fairy with Blood Red Wings had ensnared.

Its body and abdomen had the outline of a wasp, a putrid mix of dark yellow, black and red. I began to feel rather queasy myself.

Those eyes. You couldn't stop staring at them, because what you really wanted to see, wasn't there. It might be in your imagination, but it wasn't part of Darren's creative process.

Slits for eyes. A putrid sack for a body. Blood dripping from its seaweed-like wings.

Utterly horrid. Or to use Maisie's take on it, *disgusting*.

Miss McManus announced that I had won the art contest. She gave me a bag of sweets, which I shared out amongst everyone, even Darren, who seemed to have forgotten about his mid-class tantrum.

At 2:04 am, we all knew who the real winner was, yet I don't think Darren would have wished this on anyone, even the one who pipped him to the number one in art class.

It was something one boy had talked about, been laughed at, and we never saw him again. Not because the Tooth Fairy with Blood Red Wings actually *got* him, although that was our first thought.

When we had pressed Miss McManus about it, it turns out he had gone to a school for special needs, even though before the supposed creature had visited him one night, he had displayed no unusual behavior at all.

I knew he hadn't been quite right in himself that final day at school.

"First, you feel all clammy, like it's a summer's night and you can't get to sleep, though it's not - it's the dead of winter and the room should be anything but warm. The fluttering of its wings is the next thing you hear, but you don't see them. If knives and the blades of scissors could sing or whistle, that's what you would hear – a scratching sounds that made you feel like something was slicing your eyeballs off from the inside of your head. Then your legs start to feel like a deadweight, but then, like they are hardly attached to you at all. You want to get up and run, but you can't."

He had blurted it all out so fast, before stopping altogether. We added an 'and then?' but he just stopped. Actually, he vomited right in front of us, with dark green stuff coming from his gut, with things attached to them.

I know that's not the best description, but what's important to say about that is that we never saw that boy again; he went to that other school, and some weeks later his picture was on the local newspaper. He had died in mysterious circumstances. We never learned what they were, but I knew what that green stuff was now.

Seaweed.

And I knew what the little objects were attached to it.

Teeth.

Oh, how I stayed up all night waiting to see the Tooth Fairy, but Mum told me that she kept well out of sight. She had to, you see, to preserve the myth.

It seemed that her hellish counterpart had taken note of this, because I could not see the demon. I could feel something in my blood, as a little blood trickled from around my gums and teeth.

I am imagining this, I tell myself. At 2:04am, we could be forgiven for imagining anything.

The cuts feel real, and I determine that they are real. Something is cutting me from the inside of my mouth. It is then that I feel one of my teeth start to loosen. I learned in class that only the tip of my tooth is actually visible. So how much of my gum and jawbone was this demon going to cut in order to get my tooth out?

I closed one hand over my mouth, the other hand gripping Rebecca's tooth as tight as I could. I believed if I could hold on a little longer, this nightmare would be over, and I would wake up to Mum making a cup of tea and bringing me some biscuits.

The direction of the cutting device had changed, as if it was cutting a U shape in my lower gum, in order to free my tooth – or teeth, I had no idea how many the demon was going to take.

The sight of blood was enough to make me pass out, and I felt I had few options left in any case, but to surrender to the evil that surrounded me.

My head hits the pillow. I feel I have landed in a soggy mix of seaweed, sweat and blood. If I awake somehow the next day, at least I will have something interesting to tell at school.

Act 3
The Ghost of Normandy Road
Part I: The Locum

M***um was annoyed with me at first, angry at*** second, and worried for a third. Okay, I could accept that she was understandably annoyed, because I hadn't opened the door when she had knocked, not once, not twice, but three times. This referred to an earlier row I had with her about my privacy not being respected. I was ten years old, but she spent a lot of time telling me that when I was sixteen, she could no longer tell me what to do, unless I was still under her roof of course. But ask anyone – for a ten-year old, sixteen seems a lifetime away.

She had mumbled something about me being just a kid, when in other sentences she would address me as *young man*. It was difficult enough being a child without having to deal with adults who were forever changing their minds. I told her she couldn't have it both ways. She never admitted defeat, but it seemed we had agreed that 'the kid could have his privacy after all.'

She was angry when she saw that not only was I not awake and looking like I wanted to go to school, but that the bedclothes looked like they had been in a warzone for the starter, a horror movie for the main, and a psychotic chiller for dessert.

Mum had previously warned me about not eating in bed – especially things like jam doughnuts where food and jam go absolutely everywhere.

But she knew, as a mother knows, that what she was seeing was anything but jam.

My hair was a mess – that wasn't unusual in itself. I was the original bedhead. At school one day we stood at a blackboard whilst the outline of our head was drawn with white chalk.

Whoever recreated my head had drawn it crudely, but with an unhealthy dose of realism. Weren't drawings and portraits supposed to bring out the object's best features?

It looked like I had a bump on my head, and in crime programmes, they would say such a bump could only be caused by blunt force trauma.

I wasn't moving. And I was half-out of the bed too, because my clammy, seaweed-stained pillow was not something I had been able to settle on. What a night it had been.

There wasn't as much blood as I had imagined, but enough to make my normally calm mother scream – scream loud enough for me to awake from my…whatever it was.

"My God, what in the name of Jesus has gone on here?"

I could not muster an answer. I was still extremely dazed, and could barely turn my neck to answer my mother. Her hands tried to rub my shoulders to get me to arrive at a fully awake state, but instead made me shriek right in front of her. The last thing that had touched me had been that demon.

The taste of blood, rusted metal and seaweed remained in my mouth. Along with a hole – a *big* hole. I moved my tongue around the gap. I counted three whole teeth that were missing.

"My God!" My mother exclaimed again. It was irritating the first time and was getting worse with every repetition. "What happened? Tell me what happened," she said, over and over again, until I was able to provide with some kind of answer.

I forced myself to sit upright in the bed, slowly and deliberately telling my mother the truest version of events, as best as I could recall them. I noted that she was commenting on the mess, but had not asked me directly if I was okay. So I assured her I was alright. I had a monster of a headache and my mouth hurt like hell, also there was a sharp pain around my toes, but I ignored my unease for that particular moment.

Otherwise, I was keeping it all together. It could not mask the obvious – that I was shook up, extremely tired, my heart was beating faster than I would like. But I was alive, and considering the events of the night just gone, I was happy for that. In fact, talking about it with Mum seemed to make things better.

Mum resolved to do, what she always did in these kind of circumstances. She would call the priest to bless the house. I thought some kind of exorcism might be in order, but she dismissed it, and in retrospect, I would have agreed with her. It's best not to antagonise the demon in your head. The one under the bed you can just ignore.

Screw privacy. I would leave the door open from now on.

* * *

I stayed in bed for pretty much all of that day, refusing to leave it even though I knew I would have to at some point. I didn't dare to look under the bedsheet towards my toes, because something was definitely wrong, and I yet felt I had been through enough and didn't want to face another horror.

But nature called, so I knew I would have to get up. Sometimes I would lie there in the bed, hoping the urge to urinate would go away, but it never did. I could not put it off any longer. As if she possessed some kind of super sixth sense, any motion from me would be felt in the house somewhere. That would be Mum's cue to race into the bedroom formerly marked as *Private*, and she would change those bedclothes at lightning speed.

It struck me as odd that her first port of call would be a priest and not a doctor, or even the police. Mum said something about *letting sleeping dogs lie*, whatever that meant.

I forced myself into a standing position, and rocked back onto the bed. My toes were covered in balls of cotton, three toes in fact. I pulled the one cotton ball off and let out a barely disguised scream. The tips of those same three toes had been *removed*.

I examined the other two, only to find the same had been done to them. As I tried to stand on my feet, the pressure was immense, as was the pain. I could only hobble forward, but I made it to the bathroom, before vomiting again. The green seaweed came out of my mouth. *Again*.

"Mum!" I screamed. "Call a doctor!"

* * *

Mum did as she was told. A doctor did pay us a visit, but it turns out I didn't know who he was. Mum told me he was a *locum*, a word I didn't understand at the time. It was derived from Latin, as most words were, to describe 'one who holds a place.' But I wasn't to know that back then. I had a doctor I preferred to see, and especially in my own bedroom. A strange doctor wasn't welcome, so I told her so.

"I only want to see Dr McGuiness!" I complained bitterly. My mother would certainly have agreed with me, but her public face showed only one thing to this doctor – that I was being a difficult child, typical for my age.

I didn't like the doctor coming into my bedroom, but I hazily recall my screams downstairs, calling for a doctor. This situation, right now, was one of my own making.

He was about thirty-five, I guessed, maybe older. Much younger than our regular doctor. I couldn't help but say it.

"You're not Doctor McGuiness."

"No," he said, almost a bit too happily. "But I am a doctor, so I'm qualified to see to you."

That first part reminded me of Tom Baker in Doctor Who, when he encountered a mere human saying that he was a doctor. Old Tom had a witty retort back then, replying with "You may be a doctor, but I am *the* Doctor."

That was how I viewed Doctor McGuiness – a proper

Doctor, not a careerist professional only interested in a paycheck and would only want more patients on the medical roll so long as that meant more money.

The second part of this locum's statement was far more disturbing.

He was going to *'see'* to me? Whatever did that mean?

"We'll see about that," I replied. It sounded a lot harsher than I meant it to be, but I had a rough night. Just he was going to ask me things that I didn't want to tell him, not that he would believe it anyway.

"Yes we will," he replied. "Open your mouth now, Danny. Wide."

I did as I was told, at least, the will to do it was there. The pain shot right through me, and I closed my mouth again.

"Mitt burts," I mumbled incoherently.

"What did you say? I don't understand."

"Mhhiittt....mburts!" I repeated. I'm sure it sounded a lot more intelligible this time, but somehow, he remained mystified by the jumble of sounds that had escaped from my mouth.

"Ah, I see. I understand now. It *hurts* to open your mouth. Let me check something else then."

I don't know what happened. Maybe when I screamed at my mum, adrenaline had covered up the pain.

Now it was raw, unleashed, without any sense of control. I sucked my lips over and under the remaining teeth as the cold steel of the stethoscope went over my chest and back.

"Just try to breathe normally."

That was easier said than done, of course. I was at the early stages of developing bronchitis, which would lead to asthma. My thoughts raced ahead to a return to school and telling Mr Davies that my cross-country running days were over. I would try not to look too pleased about that.

He placed the stethoscope back into his box. But then he asked me to open wide again. Yes, he knew it hurt to do so. But he had to check. That was all part of being a doctor.

I tried, how I tried. But the pink gummy flesh was so raw and angry, I felt trickles of blood inside my mouth again. I thought I had opened my mouth wide enough for him to shine that yellow light of his inside it, but clearly I hadn't. His face said it all.

He called for my mother, and asked her *is he always this difficult*?

As any child would expect of their mother, she defended me – up to a point. But then she popped her head around the door and asked me to let the doctor conduct a thorough examination. *Thanks for that, Mum.* When I heard that, I was almost begging for her to send for the priest again. If the Tooth Fairy with Blood-Red Wings was to make a return, I would have hoped the priest would have had some prayer that would have banished it.

For the next five minutes, which seemed like hours, I fought the pain. I fought every urge to slam my mouth shut, and when the locum checked my toes – the missing ones, that is, I sucked my bloody tee-shirt into my mouth in order to gag my screams.

"Alright, I'm almost done here," he said. The locum went outside to talk with my mum some more, before returning back to me.

"I'm a doctor, not a fantasist," he said. "That means I don't believe in anything other than a scientific reason for things that happen. But you are the second person that I have seen with this condition. I believe the patient in question was from your school, perhaps your class, even."

My eyes widened at the revelation, but I said nothing that would betray me any further.

"As a locum, I get to travel wide in the area. I see patients that your Doctor McGuiness wouldn't necessarily get to see, you understand me? When I see injuries such as those that you have sustained, it troubles me. It troubles me a lot."

I thought I nodded in agreement, or made some gesture as if to confirm that I was listening to this locum. Due to the pain I was going through, I was no longer sure. Hazy images of the blood thirsty Tooth Fairy continued to fly in and out of my thoughts. With a buzzing sound like a hornet's nest, of course.

"That boy, the one who has the same condition as you, did not fare well at all. His parents aren't like yours. Your mother clearly loves you. As for that boy, maybe you saw some bruises on him, maybe you didn't, but he had them, I can assure you of that."

I wanted my mum to return to my room, but she could be heard pottering around in the kitchen downstairs, singing some Nana Mouskouri song. *Again.*

"It would have been so easy to call the authorities and say something like the boy's parents had been beating on him, but he had that same look at me, that you have now. As if he was trying to tell me something – something that I would not believe, because, after all, you're a child, and I am the adult. But I don't believe this sort of thing could strike twice. I regret what happened to that boy. I do not want it to happen to you. So why don't you tell me what you know?"

As he spoke to me, I felt a pain in my arm. It rose at first, as if a hot iron had been applied to my bare skin, then, the pain levelled out, and my arm felt all numb. The locum had injected me with some kind of painkiller. I felt I could talk.

"What did the boy tell you?" I asked. My words were my own again.

"He told me three things. He told me about the Witch of Hill Top Green. He told me about the Tooth Fairy with Blood-Red Wings. You already know the third."

I looked at him. I wondered if he could be trusted. But he had done something I could not believe. He had actually mentioned the Tooth Fairy with Blood Red Wings.

"Of course, Brian Burley was the Witch of Hill Top Green. You probably read about it in the newspapers. A wicked man, who preyed on schoolchildren. No actual Witch, so no mystery."

I found myself nodding again.

"The Tooth Fairy with Blood-Red Wings has a name too."

"What's her name?" I blurted out my request too quickly, and I felt another tooth loosen."

"Not she. Not he. It's the kind of creature that does not have a gender. You know it too, because it serves the Devil. Its name is *Seta*."

It was just a word, but my heart raced to a hundred once it had left his lips. The hateful name just hung in the air. I wanted it to go away. I wanted the locum to go away.

"Mum!" I shouted.

The singing stopped and the staircase started to be hammered as she made her ascent.

"Alright, I'll be going now. But you had better give Seta what it wants. You know what I'm on about."

Mum popped her head around the door. "Everything alright, pet?" she asked me.

I nodded again. My, how stupid I must have looked, with bandaged toes, a swollen arm, a bloodied mouth and my toy dog nodding head.

"You said *three* things," I spoke to the locum, and I realised my tone was accusatory. It appeared to have taken him by surprise.

"Normandy Road," he said gruffly.

"What of it?" asked my mother.

"It's where I'm off to next," he said brightly.

I sat upright in my bed with my arms folded in defiance. He knew full well what he was on about, and so did I. Also, I didn't happen to believe his *Brian Burley* story. The Witch was real, because the Tooth Fairy was real. With the mention of this word, Seta – he had all but confirmed it.

I felt under my pillow. The small object was still there. I would not under any circumstances let Rebecca's tooth leave my possession. She had entrusted it to me. Granted, it was more unusual than her last gift, which had been a simple hairpin. But it was worth all the treasure in the world to me.

It troubled me greatly that the locum had seen the other boy too, at least; he *claimed* to have seen him.

I would rest for the day, but somehow, I had to see Rebecca. I had to make sure that she didn't end up living next to that house on Normandy Road.

I would have all day to put a plan of action together. Somehow, I would have to convince Mum to let me go into school the very next day.

* * *

My mind was willing, my body was not, and more than that, Mum was insistent – I would not be going to school that day, or for many days thereafter.

I was so worried about Rebecca. There was no real way of contacting her. Yes, we had a home phone, but I didn't have Rebecca's number. I could not conceive of any scenario whereby Mum would let me use the phone.

In fact, the home seemed to be full of all kinds of things that were too expensive to use. There was the inevitable drama of electric bills, gas bills, phone bills and others when the brown envelopes would land on the mat. Somewhere in the house, the fallout had already begun.

For my own part, I hardly watched television, listened to the radio, or phoned anyone. More accurately, there was no-one to phone, and in any case, I would only want to call Rebecca.

With few options open to me, I took the one that was available, absorbing as many books as I could at Birchfield Library. The problem now was that I couldn't realistically make it to that haven of literature. There was also a bigger problem, as the hours ticked by and late evening approached.

I wondered if I would be visited again by *Seta*.

I wondered if Seta actually feared anything.

I wondered how I was going to stay awake all night to protect Rebecca's tooth.

While I was thinking about all that, I actually did fall asleep.

* * *

Four days passed without incident, and suddenly I found myself at the weekend. I had resisted putting much weight onto my foot, but the pain had definitely subsided. That didn't mean I wasn't suffering, I was hobbling around a lot, like the time my brother broke his leg playing football. He wasn't very tall, no more than 5'7", and gained something of a reputation as a dirty player. Opponents on the field nicknamed him 'The Animal.' If you ask me, he got what was coming to him.

My mother wanted help with the shopping, so she was glad to see me up and about, even if I wasn't operating at my very best.

Often, we would bump into other people my mum would know. I would have to endure the usual comments, such as *Hasn't he grown? Aww, he's grown so big!* Plus, there was my personal favourite, *He'll be grown up and left home before you know it.*

Yes, I did want to be grown up. If I was, perhaps I wouldn't be so scared of the demons in the grassland beyond the school, the tooth demon (because that's what it was), or one particular red-bricked house.

The gossiping between the adults went on for an age, and it was at that moment, the one between me wishing a hole to open up in the ground and swallow me whole, and forcing my fingers to dig the concrete up, that I saw her.

Actually, she saw me first.

"Rebecca!"

My mum told me not to shout in public, but I didn't care. I hobbled towards her. My mum took a hypocritical stance and decided to shout in public after me. But I could no longer hear her. Anything she said was like an echo.

I could see Rebecca in front of me, and that was all that mattered.

I got to her much quicker than my damaged limbs would have wanted me to.

"Rebecca----I'm so happy to see you."

"You too, Danny," she replied. "You've been having a rough time of it. I'm so sorry. I can take that tooth back off you if you've still got it."

I had still got it, of course I had. My mind wasn't processing things very well, because here was Rebecca saying she would have the tooth back, and I really did want to return it. But I felt I could cope with that hated Tooth demon if I could see Rebecca on a regular basis. I did not want him to harm her.

"I don't have it on me, Rebecca. It's at home. I'm sorry."

This was to be my first lie to Rebecca. She looked at me as if to say that she understood, but I felt her expression saw right through me.

"When will you be back at school?"

"I hope on Monday," I replied. I really did hope so too.

"I might not be," she said, and her words immediately saddened me. "I might have other things to do, you know."

Yeah, I knew. Like moving into that house. I knew it wasn't the actual house, but still, it was close enough. Why was she agreeing to this? Oh yes – it was because we were children, and as such, we had no say in anything.

I looked over at my mother, who was still chatting to that woman. Turning back to Rebecca, she smiled at me. We kissed several times and I thought if I died right there and then, that would be okay. Kissing in public. I would never have thought it possible of myself, or Rebecca for that matter.

Before I knew it, she had pulled away from me, saying that she had to go.

No problem. I was determined to see her again on the following Monday.

Act 3
The Ghost of Normandy Road Part II: The First Night

Somehow, I had made it to school, but there was no sign of Rebecca. I asked some of the girls, but they said I didn't know what I was on about. Perhaps I shouldn't have been surprised, because Rebecca was much like myself – we didn't mix easily with others.

All the same, it seemed very strange. Rebecca seemed quite insistent that she would be there at school, and I had made an especial effort to return.

When I didn't see her, I was utterly crestfallen.

I also had to deal with some of the boys who mocked my walk. Miss McManus would tell them off, but outside of class, they would start their mocking routine once again.

"You know, that boy walked a bit like that, just before he had to leave our school," one of them said. "Maybe that's what will happen to you!"

I tried to ignore it, but the insults hurt. I looked at my watch. Two and a half-hours to go. Once the school bell rang, it did not matter if I ran, or if I hobbled. I would go and find Rebecca. I would go to that house on Normandy Road. It was so much easier to be brave, when I didn't actually have to face such a tricky task at that particular moment.

"The Tooth Fairy with Blood-Red Wings got to you, right?" said one of the boys.

I ignored the boy, and the laughs of both him and his friends.

"Probably got to her too," said another. "Oh Rebecca! I love you. Wanna kiss you! Again, and again and again. Mwah! Mwah! Mwah!"

The boys made kissing sounds with their mouths. I wanted to punch them. Instead, I gave the weakest of responses.

"Just stop it, will you?"

My voice sounded all wrong…the pitch was far too high, and the group seized on it.

"No wonder you're shouting a girl's name all the time. You sound like one. Maybe we should call you *Rebecca*."

That was *it* for me. I swung a fist at the one boy, but I was too slow. He wasn't; ducking below my arm before producing a fist that seemed to come out of nowhere.

I was dizzy on the ground. I could hear a reassuring voice somewhere in the distance. I had heard my mum talk about the tunnel of light we go through when we die. Had he really hit me that hard?

"Hey, what's this?"

That was the menacing voice of one of the boys. He kicked out at whatever it was, before picking it up and unravelling the material around it.

"Urghh! It's a tooth!"

"*I told you he was weird*," said another. "What kind of freak would carry a tooth around with him?"

From somewhere deep inside, I found my voice and the aggression to take him on. The fact I was outnumbered at the time didn't enter into my head.

"Give me that!" I shouted. I *demanded*. "You better give it to me, or-"

In time, I would realise that less talk, more action was better. They already had a plan for me. I was learning on the go, and so I was a step or several steps behind them, each and every time.

"Oh, I'll give it to you, alright."

I felt a pain on my outstretched arm which had tried in vain to retrieve the object. The boy was standing on my arm, and as he was much fatter and heavier than me, I could not free it.

"I'll give it back to you, if you do something for us."

I didn't want to do anything for them. I have never wanted to be in the safety of my own home, tucked into my small bed more than at any point in my life. It's funny how we don't appreciate these little things. One thing was for sure – I would not do any deals with these thugs. I'd get my revenge on them somehow. This, I vowed.

"*What*?"

"That's simple. Visit the house on Normandy Road late at night, and wait until the ghost appears."

“There’s no ghost! There’s no ghost-” I screamed, but he put so much pressure on my arm, I mouthed something about an *okay*. I would just have to do it.

I would just have to face my fears and beat them. *Easy*.

“I’ll be watching you,” he said. “I live in the building opposite that house. *I’ve seen her*. Oh yeah, I’ve seen her. But I know better than to go inside. Those three boys, what a shame, no-one ever heard anything about them again. Maybe you’ll break the curse, who knows? She might just take a liking to you.”

I hated this dough-shaped kid, and I promised myself that if I got out of that house without suffering any harm, he would be the first to feel my fists.

“Don’t you lose that tooth, otherwise I might just bring that ghost over with me to see you. Or maybe I will bring the witch. And if you don’t have that tooth when I come for it, I’ll do some damage to you that you won’t walk away from.”

I turned away from the group and tried my best not to hobble. Stand tall, shoulders back, I kept telling myself. I would not let them see me any more humbled than I already felt.

* * *

The hours clicked by, and the blue light in the sky began to give way to a greyish, overcast haze. But of course, this was how it was meant to be. The house wouldn’t have it any other way. It was living, breathing, existing both in our time and outside of it. If I was meant to escape it, it would only be because the house had further use for me. Or weirdly, perhaps no further use for me. I was not happy about either option.

At home, things seemed to be working out in my favour. Mum had left me a note saying she would be working late, but she would bring me back a cake from the shop.

I was confident that this would be a cake I could handle, and would not feel guilty about. My adrenaline had been high all day, and I was burning off fat through pure worry.

It was only four o'clock, and yet already the clouds had gathered, choking the light out of the sky. Then, the darkness would fall on top, and with it, taking any remnant of hope I would have for the evening.

My beautiful Rebecca still invaded my thoughts. It was not like her just to disappear like that. I could not stop thinking about her, and I was actually grateful, because it was the thought of her that kept me going. In my back pocket, I still had her hairpin. I checked it and smoothed a finger on the outline. That wasn't reassuring enough for me, so I removed it gently from my pocket.

It was green in colour, an unusual choice given that most of the girls who wore hairpins chose pink, red, or sometimes purple. But the green went well with Rebecca's reddish hair, which to me often looked golden in the sun. Green wasn't my favourite colour. In fact, you could say I disliked green more than any other colour, because I had bad recollections about it. Then, when I was given this by Rebecca, my opinion about it changed almost instantly.

There was something else. Something looked a bit different about the hairpin this time. It looked a bit rusty, and yet I wondered how this could have happened.

If I couldn't look after her hairpin, how could I look after her tooth? Oh wait…the tooth has already gone, and with that thought, the sickness in my stomach had returned. How could I look after her? And did she need me to do so anyway?

Five o'clock.

I began to think, albeit belatedly, about the logistics of this folly. For that boy to see me, it wouldn't be enough just to cross over the threshold into the house. I would have to traverse the stairs, that looked like they would break at the slightest amount of weight being put upon them.

I could not think about the other factor – even if there was no problem at the house itself, I didn't trust that boy just to give up the tooth; and I simply had to have it back. Even if he broke every bone in my body, I had to have it back. The question was – what was he prepared to do in order to hang onto it? When tested, such bullies tend to crumble. Boy, would I be happy to see him crumble!

Five o'clock was here and gone. I must have dozed off, because when I awoke, it was 6:30pm. I hobbled from my bed, and outside, the darkness had fallen, but not completely set. I would have to get moving.

The painkillers the locum gave me had worked, but I took an extra dose because I just had to – it was the only way to get through this.

There was an after effect that I found myself suffering from, and it was a sense of unreality around me. My senses were dulled somewhat. I had shut the door, and believed I had locked it behind me; as it was often one of those things we worry about, but tend to do automatically.

From our house, we would walk up Aston Lane, turn left into Stoneleigh Road, and keep going until Normandy Road opened up ahead.

The red brick house was to the right of me. With all my heart I wanted to turn left, towards Rebecca's house, or turn back, and go home. But there was a light in the house behind me, and opposite the big house itself. He was telling the truth, he lived directly opposite the very house I didn't want to go into.

He switched the bedroom light off, and shone a torch under his chin. The scene gave him a rather macabre, sinister look, and – dare I say, I felt a touch of evil about him. What a creep.

In his other hand, his thumb and forefinger grasped Rebecca's tooth. I felt pretty disgusted that he had a hold of something that was so precious to me.

He shook his head at me as if to say I would not see it again, or Rebecca, if I didn't do his bidding. I don't think he understood who he was dealing with. I was going to survive the house – somehow. And when I was done, I would go and see him, and rip the tooth out of his dead hands. If that's what it took, then that's what I would have to do. This was my Rebecca we were talking about.

I couldn't bear to look at him a single second longer, so turned away from him. In many ways, he represented the rational side of the evil that was in front of me. I knew there was something evil in that house, but until I saw it or felt it, the fear itself was irrational, and I couldn't let it stop me from moving forward.

Whilst I looked in that boy's direction, the fact was that it delayed the inevitable. I was grateful he still had the tooth, I supposed.

I crossed over into the front garden, passing the brickwork that protected the garden, though not that well in my opinion. The ground was soft in parts, due to moss that had grown through the cracks on the concrete.

Despite me wearing thick jeans, weeds nicked at my legs. I could feel the sharpest of thorns and nettles poking through. But who was I kidding? Weeds and thorns were the least of my problems. I just had to keep my mind on the task ahead.

On approach to the entrance, the house looked cold, uninviting and did all it could to repel me. I knew it did not want me to enter, and I also felt that it would make me pay for doing so. But again, I had to do it. I'd walk through walls for Rebecca. I would drag my naked body over broken glass for her. There wasn't a single thing you could name that I would not do for her, except for one thing perhaps. I know you might think it was silly, but that one thing was – I could not give her up. I could not stop loving her. This was a forever kind of thing for me. Even though I was about to go through one of the most hellish experiences of my life, thoughts of Rebecca made it easier for me to cope, confident in the knowledge that I would see her again.

The main door, which had been a vibrant shade of red at one time, had faded to a dirty, discoloured rusty shade.

A strong draft emerged from the front door, hitting me in the face. The odour was strange, in that the air seemed trapped inside from days long gone. I remember a place local to us, a building from the Jacobean period that was known as *Aston Hall*. I had been in it a few times, and they actually ran an event every two years at Halloween called Aston Hall by Candlelight.

That place seemed to emit the same kind of odour. Sometimes it was hard to make the distinction between a deathly odour and a merely ancient one.

One, two and *three* more steps, and I would be inside. I recall one of the stewards at Aston Hall telling me that the highest area in the place was witness to a hanging – one of the servants had killed themselves, and that – along with other ghosts, were said to roam the Hall.

I was intrigued at the time, but remained sufficiently scared enough to stay out of the place – *especially* at Halloween.

For all I knew, Normandy Road wasn't haunted at all. We had been up and down it lots of times. Kids often told each other scare stories and I wouldn't be telling the truth if I said I never wanted to hear one.

I decided not to let the fears overcome me. I would stay rational about this.

I stood directly underneath the threshold now, and the archway above my small and slender frame quizzed me; testing if I really wanted to go through with this.

No, I don't want to go through with this. But I have to.

I stepped inside, and I heard, or more accurately – felt something. The door didn't do what you'd expect – slam shut behind me as in the horror movies, no – it actually clung to the hinge on the door, as if for dear life. Could a door breathe? I began to consider the possibility.

Inside the hallway, I could not feel the draft of air behind me anymore. This house certainly seemed strange, and appeared to be not of the modern time. I had no idea for how long it had been vacated, but I would have guessed at maybe fifteen or twenty years. But at my age, it was hard to make an informed guess.

Two huge portraits hung on either side of the room. One was of a man, again, I'm guessing, but it looked like he was wearing a grand costume from Victorian times. On the right- hand side, the portrait was of two men, small in size, like dwarfs or something like that. They appeared to be haggling over the price of something, or someone. This picture drew my gaze more than the first. There was a girl in the picture too, standing upright behind a table. She was wearing a necklace.

I was shaken out of my stumbling excuse for a walk by the fact I had hit wood – I had bumped into the staircase and grazed my chin. My look returned to the girl in the picture. The two men looked to have changed expression, and were more animated this time. Speaking of *Time*, there was an hourglass on the table. Right now, the sand was at the top, but I could have sworn it was moving into its other half at the bottom, right in front of my very eyes. The very notion of oxygen seemed to have been sucked right out of the room. My heart beat faster and my chest felt like it could no longer function properly. This was the last place on earth to have a palpitation. I've had them before, so you might think palpitation is a big word for little me, but once you have had one, you learn what it is and you never forget what it is.

My head turned swiftly back to the portrait of the man behind me. I had only applied scant observation before, but I could see whilst for the most part, it looked the same, there were now some alarming differences.

When I looked at it originally, I could have sworn he was a fair-haired man of about twenty, his portraiture was displayed in his left profile. He had narrow blue eyes, his skin exemplified his youth and lack of experience of the world. Every wrinkle on someone was meant to signify a pain that could never be washed away. This man had none of that.

This *new* portrait was far more disturbing. The eyes were larger and black. The mouth was pursed in an accusatory manner. His eyebrows were full and thick.

His hair was black, thick, wild *and* unkempt. There was something else too - the figure was looking directly at me.

If I didn't know better, I would have believed that the boy from across the road had somehow switched the portraits in a bid to unnerve me still further.

That was impossible of course, how could anyone do that? Still, it didn't explain what had just occurred. Yes, I was upset and very nervous. But all I had to do, was go up the stairs, onto the first floor, and maybe the second. Just enough for that boy to see me from his bedroom window. I had no evidence he was still looking. He could have just flopped onto his bed and put his stereo on. Then, when he did not see me, he could throw Rebecca's tooth away or do whatever with it, and there was not a damned thing I could do about it. I really hated being powerless. One day, I intended to be one of the most powerful people of all.

First things first though. If he was still looking out of the window, he would gesture back, presumably with Rebecca's tooth in his hand, and then, I could run out of that house as if the Devil himself was behind me.

If I had any energy left, I would use it to kick his front door in and get the tooth back. There would be no second night in the place, that much I had promised myself,

Oh God. Maybe the eyes in the portraits were moving, maybe they weren't, but I made my way up the stairs anyway. The stairs were not completely bare. A thin bit of carpet ran up the middle of the stairwell, frayed and worn by years of neglect. I thought the original colour was blue, with tints of gold strands. It might have had a discernable pattern at one time, but I could not make it out now.

The stairs felt soft, like the consistency of marshmallows, and I was sure that, any second now, I would fall through, hit the bottom – whatever that was, and be forever a part of the house.

Negative thoughts hold us back, so I decided to press on. I counted the stairs of course, and it was a higher staircase than the one back home. Home, where my safety was. Why was I doing this again?

Oh yes. *Rebecca*, that's why.

I counted seventeen steps in all, and now, I stood above the two supernatural paintings. I didn't want to consider the return trip down the steps, as I was already up quite a height. Maybe I could slide down the bannister, who knows?

I chastised myself for letting my mind race ahead. I would have to deal with one thing at a time.

There was another gust of damp air that breezed passed me – or more accurately, passed through me. I now believed I knew what kind of air this was. Sometimes, a body would be exhumed from a grave, and I bet that scent would be the first to greet those doing the exhumation.

There were more portraits to the right and to the left of me. But these had suffered the worst of the decay. I could be forgiven for saying that they had been willingly defaced, and I could be absolutely right too, as eyes had been ripped out of the paintings, leaving gaping, black holes in their stead.

If it had been a portrait of a woman, a liquid that looked like blood had been smeared across her chest. Where the object of the portrait was a male, a thin but definitive red line had been drawn across the throat, and the area by the heart had been torn out, with the canvas left abused like a hangnail.

Several rooms lay ahead. If I turned to the ones on the right, I believed the boy across the road would be able to see me. I walked slowly but purposely towards the first door on the right, encircled my hand around the doorknob, and hoped it would unlock.

* * *

The door was stiff, and warped from age, wear and neglect. I tried with all my might to shift it, but it would not budge, even though it had made a clicking sound when I turned the doorknob.

I stood back, and kicked at the door but this seemed to make the wood snag at the doorframe with an unspoken determination to remain out of bounds for me.

Fine. I would have to try the second door.

Up ahead, something stopped me in my tracks. There was a window at the northernmost point, adorned with a thick curtain netting behind a lavish drape of velvet.

In front of the window was something I believed to be a floor lamp of some kind. It was covered with some material, like chiffon from a wedding dress. But then, I could hear a voice emanating from the shape. And it was moving in my direction.

A girl's voice asked me, "Why are you here? You shouldn't be here."

Jesus Christ. That was all the motivation I needed to get out of there.

I don't remember negotiating the stairs, but whether I jumped all seventeen steps or slid down the bannister or not, I hightailed it out of the building.

I looked up at the opposing window. The boy was there, laughing at me, the little bastard. He opened his window, and held the object I believed that was Rebecca's tooth in his hand, and prepared to drop it towards the undergrowth surrounding his house.

I wanted to scream 'No' but nothing would come out from my mouth. Then, behind him, I saw *It*. Saw *Her*.

The same shape I had seen in the house just now. He was oblivious as she placed a hand on his neck, and using a knife with the other, slit his throat whilst his mouth was still open and laughing at me.

This time, I really did scream.

But the light had gone out from the window. The figure and the boy were gone, and with it, any hope of recovering Rebecca's tooth.

What the hell had my meddling unleashed?

Act 3
The Ghost of Normandy Road Part III: The Second Night

T***hankfully, Mum didn't do her usual quiz round of*** *Twenty Questions* when I arrived home. She thought I was going through another of my *phases,* which I found myself agreeing with, at least, *in part* I did.

She had brought me a cup of tea, and through my delirious state, she could make out the word *Rebecca* and yet asked me nothing further. I could hear her muttering to herself about calling the doctor to come and see me.

I think I mumbled something back about *Any doctor but the Locum* and that was all I remembered.

I had to find Rebecca, but I would also have to find that boy, even though I disliked him intensely. Whatever happened to him must have been my imagination in overdrive.

I had wanted him to have some misfortune for forcing me into this situation, but to die so horribly like that? No, I did not want that at all.

My sleep was disturbed too. Images of The Witch of Hill Top Green, plus The Tooth Fairy with Blood-Red Wings, continued to attack me. But now there was a new entity to be scared of. Actually my hatred of that boy had changed once I had come into contact with that ghost. I felt both a pity and an empathy I did not think was possible.

Was the ghost just taking advantage of the situation? Was it connected to the tooth somehow, or the hated Tooth Demon itself? Were they one and the same?

I had no idea. Whilst these questions filled my head, I fell asleep. It had been a good rest, and I surprised my mum, not for the first time that week, by leaving early for school.

* * *

It was 8:20am when I arrived. Sometimes I would play football with the kids or chat with the girls. Since getting to know Rebecca, I only looked on other girls as friends. She was all I wanted in a girl, and yet she wasn't to be found.

"Rebecca? You know her, I know you do."

One of the girls looked confused at me.

"What does she look like? I know lots of girls, just maybe not all of their names."

That was a fair enough statement. Even the teachers used a register for the children's names in the morning roll call. I for one didn't know all the names of the boys. But I had seen Rebecca with this particular group of girls. However, she continued to be a little too evasive for my liking. I described how Rebecca looked – red hair that looked gave the appearance of golden honey in the sunshine, rosy cheeks. Freckles. Pale skin. Or maybe it was her rosy cheeks that gave her that complexion. Always wore dresses with a floral print, and if it was cold, a cardigan with her favourite colour of green.

"Yeah, well, I think I've seen her. Oh wait!"

She shouted out *Rebecca* at the top of her voice, and I turned around, my smile already geekily prepared.

But it wasn't her. A girl was approaching, but it wasn't her.

"Have you seen Rebecca? He, um – sorry, what's your name? I'm terrible with names!"

"Danny," I mumbled, before getting back to the more important subject matter. "You would know her if you saw her. She's very beautiful."

The words just escaped from me, I didn't mean them to. But girls could be even crueler than boys. Their impish giggling annoyed me, but it was my fault. I sheepishly walked away.

The girl I was speaking to – and I didn't recall her name either, then said something that chilled me.

"Maybe she's gone to that special school, you know. Like where that boy went. Maybe you should look there instead."

I felt mortified. There had to be answers to questions my small mind had not yet the intelligence to ask.

It was true, children did leave and go to other schools. There was nothing sinister about that; Mum had told me so herself, especially when there had been another *Rebecca* incident.

"All the talk of this new girl. May I remind you how desperately in love you were with that other girl before? Sarah…wasn't that her name?"

She was right. Maybe I was too quick in matters of the heart, matters I was too young to fully comprehend. Maybe her name was Sarah, maybe it was something else. I felt ashamed of myself for not knowing. Mum told me that I would meet someone else one day, and forget about Rebecca, just as I had forgotten about Sarah.

Also missing from school that day was Miss McManus. Miss Oakley just wasn't the same, and so I avoided asking her anything about Rebecca, Miss McManus or anyone else for that matter.

Class was unusual in that it was quiet, orderly, and functional. It wasn't uncommon for Miss Oakley to run very tight ship, though we would have all agreed that Miss McManus got the best out of us. Mis Oakley's classes were only memorable for their dryness. We could remember little of what we were actually taught, so frightened as we were of Miss Oakley.

It was a Friday, and I was resigned to perhaps having to get through a weekend not knowing if Miss McManus was ill or not – or something worse. I scratched thoughts from my head that she had been taken by the same force that now held Rebecca, and also that awful boy.

As gross as it would have appeared to some, I felt lost without Rebecca's tooth. I checked my back pocket again, and yes – her hairpin was still there.

Without even thinking about it, I took her hairpin out and pressed it to my lips. It had rusted, and perhaps its condition had worsened since I had last checked on it, but it belonged to her and now I was its keeper. Not its owner. When I saw her again, I would be sure to return it.

As we laboured towards home-time and 3:20pm, with both Rebecca and Miss McManus nowhere to be seen, I turned my head to look out of the window.

Actually, I *heard* the sound before seeing the one who was creating it.

A girl, wearing a floral print dress, white socks and red shoes was holding a bag, like one of those huge postal bags that contained letters. Inside was a football, I was guessing, because she would drop it to the floor, and then pick the bag up again.

She had her back to me, and yet I knew something wasn't *of the day* about her. Why would a girl be left to wander the school playground on her own?

She kept picking up the bag, and dropping it, until she was certain someone was looking in her direction. She felt it – I did too.

The bag did not contain a football, as I first thought, though the shape was still round.

I recognised it. It belonged to the boy who had gone to that school, and had never been seen again by any of us.

It was a human head, with its eyes gouged out and its mouth ripped to one side. The macabre design of a smile appeared deliberate, designed to shock and it had worked.

I was screaming at the window. Miss Oakley did all she could to calm me down, but all I could was watch as my white shirt became peppered with blotches of red. Maybe it was the rusting hairpin, maybe it was the shock of seeing the events unfold as they did in the playground, but something shook me out of my state.

There was the unmistakeable sting of a hand across my face. Miss Oakley had hit me.

"You'll pay," she said coldly. "You'll pay for what you did."

She gripped my arm by the muscle just under my right shoulder, squeezing so hard I think my skin would turn purple. With her other hand, she hit me again and again. The trickle of blood had become a stream.

In the end, the girl I had been talking to about Rebecca's whereabouts had somehow pulled Miss Oakley from me, and stood between us.

"Hit him again. But you'll have to hit me too. We're not going to lose him to that place like the others. Hit him again, and I'll make sure you're going there anyway."

There was an uneasy standoff as Miss Oakley was clearly not acting like herself. She surveyed the situation – children looking on in horror at her, whilst this defiant little girl, whose name I did not know before that day, was shielding me from harm. It should have been something to be ashamed of – a girl protecting me, but then other children stood up beside her in solidarity.

"I will retire to the Head's Office," said Miss Oakley, any fight that had been inexplicably within her had gone, along with her voice.

The following week, when we would return for school, Miss Oakley had taken her formal retirement. We would not be seeing her again.

* * *

I returned to school on Monday, much to the surprise of my mother. I wasn't traumatised by that particular event. I still had Rebecca, and only Rebecca, on my mind.

The blood hadn't actually been that bad. But the report of a teacher repeatedly hitting a child had made the local evening newspaper, and the Head was on television to apologise profusely.

When questioned about Miss Oakley's out of character behaviour, he had no answers. Once again, he apologised to me, my mother, and reaffirmed that all the children at the school were safe, and would always be safe. That was a hell of a statement to make, considering what was half a mile away in Normandy Road.

A whole week had gone by, and the boy was nowhere to be seen.

I looked up at his home, and the light in the bedroom was on, but the rooms downstairs were in complete darkness.

"*Hello*?" I shouted. My lips and mouth were still healing. "Hello?" I tried once more.

I knocked on the door. I didn't care how stupid my next sentence sounded.

"Give me back the tooth! I did what you asked me to do! Now give it back. *Give it back*!"

I banged on the door relentlessly until finally, there was an answer. It was an old man, easily double my mother's age.

"What in the name of God do you want?"

"I'm sorry." I attempted to catch my breath, as the exertion had clearly taken all my energy. "A boy that lives here goes to my school. He has something of mine."

The old man stood back inside his hallway. "We're just preparing his room. I don't suppose they told you – well, it doesn't matter now I suppose. Wait a moment, will you?"

I nodded. Even though the rain started to hammer down, I waited outside. There was a smell of incense in the house. In the darkened room next door I could hear someone talking.

Actually, the person was saying prayers, and asking God to help the family at *this difficult time*.

"I saw you on the news," said the man, who had returned. "You had best be careful, you know. The mind can deceive us all. Never mind the *mind over matter*. All that matters to any of us, is to know what is *real*. That is what keeps us safe in this world, and keeps bad people from doing bad things."

I mulled over his cryptic words. I knew some big words, and there were some words that kids younger than me understood, and I didn't. I'd have time to catch up, I supposed.

"Am I supposed to understand any of that?"

"Whether you do or not is a matter for *you* alone. Just remember that I told you." The man produced a white envelope from inside his suit pocket. He was wearing black, and I had noticed some of the people inside were wearing black too.

"I believe that *this* belongs to you."

I thanked him without knowing truly what I had thanked him for, and because it was raining, I placed the envelope and its contents inside my coat pocket, and ran home as fast as I could. But it had to be the tooth. I didn't ask him how he got it, or what state the boy was in when he did find it. I was just glad to have it back. I have never been so glad to have something back in my life. That little tooth of Rebecca's meant everything to me.

Mum was there to greet me at the door.

"Are you alright?"

"Yeah, I'm fine."

"The doctor dropped by and left you some medicine. He said you're to take them as soon as possible."

I counted four bottles of tablets, one tube of ointment, and a huge bottle of medicine. My stomach was tiny, and rumbled in disapproval.

"I'm to have all *this*?"

"Not straight away, darling. Do you want me to read the labels to you?"

I told her I could manage that just fine. There was, however, one thing I did want to know.

"Who brought these? The doctor, or the locum?"

"What's the difference? They are both doctors."

Oh no, Mum - there's a difference. There really is.

"Mum?"

"Dr McGuiness brought them."

She spoke in a clipped tone that was supposed to demonstrate her matriarchal authority to me. Instead, I knew she was lying. Ironic, considering she was the first person to tell me that I should never tell lies.

I decided to play along and gathered up the meds. She knew I would just go to my room and stew for a while, but she was wrong. I wanted to know what was in that envelope. From its bulge I could tell it was more than just a piece of paper.

I shut the door with my foot, and it slammed louder than I meant it to. Still, what was done, was done.

I placed the medicines under my bed. If the locum brought them, and nothing would shift my opinion that he did, then I was having no part of his medicinal help. For all I knew, he wanted to kill me.

My foot still hurt, but as time had passed, I could put my weight on it without many problems. My balance was much improved too, as I had to work on it. It was bad before the Tooth Fairy had attacked me, so it could only get better with practise.

Yes, I had decided to just call it the Tooth Fairy again; by calling it a Demon, I think I had possibly invoked something evil and unpleasant. I decided to play it safe. I could hear my mother saying *Not before time*.

I felt strangely comforted to know that Rebecca's tooth was now back in my possession. Okay, so I hadn't opened the envelope just yet, but it had to be that. What else could it possibly be? It wasn't like Christmas, where a carefully wrapped present would reveal a wonder so amazing, I would cherish it forever, only to be let down by the truth when I saw the reality of what it was, and so my dreams were crushed. I had a lot of Christmases like that, and until Rebecca came along, I cared little about life or myself.

I opened it carefully, turned the open end towards my bed, and sure enough, it fell out onto the bedclothes.

Rebecca's tooth.

What happened to the boy, I did not know, and in that moment, I did not care. I should have washed it, I know, but I was so overcome to see it again, I kissed her tooth.

Then, feeling slightly disgusted because I knew it had been in that boy's hand, I ran to the bathroom and rinsed my mouth out. I could hear exclamations from the kitchen. My mum knew I hated mouthwash.

I poured some water over Rebecca's tooth as well, attempting to sanitise it in some way. I picked up a few cotton wool balls and placed the tooth amongst them.

Now it was completely safe.

I went back into the bedroom, and something else poked out of the envelope.

It was a piece of paper with a drawing on it.

It was crude, to say the least, but that boy, like myself, was just ten years old. One could hardly expect a Rembrandt.

The image was of himself, I guessed. Around him was the window frame from which he had stood mocking me.

A red crayon had been drawn across his throat. Girlish kisses, marked by a small x on the far left of the red line, and also to the right of it, made it look strange. *So strange.*

In the top left corner, was a drawing of another boy. His face had been coloured in black, with blue crayon strands like tears from his eyes. That was because something around him was making him weep.

Above him in the top left-hand corner, was an arrow pointing upwards.

As there was nothing to point up to, I turned the page over.

The horrific image of the Tooth Fairy with Blood-Red Wings had been drawn; masterfully so, and certainly good enough for Rembrandt to have been its creator.

Huge bulbous eyes with slits for irises. Wings stained with blood. A pulpy, wasp-like abdomen. It was hovered over a street, a street which had been so faithfully created, and so accurately depicted; that it could only be Normandy Road.

I took a huge intake of breath and turned the sheet of paper over again. The amateur drawing of the boy was almost a surreal kind of comfort to me.

But every single stroke of the crayon had been meant.

To the left of the boy with the red line across his throat was the image of a girl. The hair colour was a mesh of red and honey blonde. She had a narrow chin, big blue eyes, and the thinnest of lips. If I could look closer, and for longer, I would have said that the lips joined together, almost as if they were *stitched* together as a deliberate act.

My mum said the same about women who wore headscarves on a summer's day, or men who wore beards and glasses.

This was just a drawing, and yet, not just a drawing. I felt it was a living, breathing *thing* – and the same creator that made the portraits move in that house – surely, this was another from that macabre collection.

I threw the paper hurriedly to the bed. My first thought was to tear it apart, then, for whatever reasoning took a hold of me, I decided against doing that.

It just sat on top of my bedclothes, daring me to pick it up again.

The girl's big blue eyes remained large, but had darkened. It was no trick of the light. It was actually happening in front of me.

No answers could be found here. I would have to go back to that house.

* * *

Mum shouted after me, saying that I should rest my legs and recover a while longer. But if I rested any longer, there may not be a 'me' to see in the next day. As much as I did not want to go back to the house, it was there that answers would be found.

That boy had gone to a 'special school,' Miss McManus had taken time off from school for the first time ever that I or any of us could recall, Miss Oakley had stepped up to a new level of craziness – even for her. Now the boy who had dared me, were nowhere to be seen.

That left the most precious thing of all to me in this world – *Rebecca,* who was also nowhere to be seen.

Evil in the house be damned, I told myself as I made me way to Normandy Road. It was easier to feel more confident on the outside, wasn't it?

Fortune favours the brave, so they say. I felt many emotions as I approached the familiar red-bricked building, but being brave was not one of them.

I saw a few people on the approach, but I could not be deterred from my task. It was a group of adults in their forties or fifties I would guess. I could smell alcohol on the group – they obviously had been sampling their own bar in the house before hitting the pubs.

"I wouldn't go in there," shouted one of them tipsily.

"Yeah, there's all manner of horrors in there, little boy."

Still another shouted after me.

"Evil preys on the innocent."

That last statement was said without a hiccup or a drunken slur. I turned around, trying to make out which of them said it. I could not tell, and I did not want to waste time in trying to find out. They were just trying to scare me. Well, they had failed. I was already scared by the time they had thrown their drunken slurs in my direction.

I covered my ears, and ran up the stairs in the house. I was looking for that girl. I did not want to see her, but I had to see her. I just had to. She was the key to all this. I was convinced of her secret. She was the Ghost of Normandy Road.

* * *

As I ascended to the second level, a sinister vision fed my eyes. All the doors that had been previously locked were open, and fully ajar.

I passed one, then another, then *another*. All open. All with that scent of the dead. Damp, earthen, claustrophobic. All waiting to claim its next victim.

Jesus God, help me. I wasn't sure if I believed those words. But Mum certainly did, and blessed herself for good measure. I made sure that I did the same.

"Hello?"

That was stupid, so stupid of me. What did I want to happen next, exactly?

"Hello, right back at you. Why don't we have a nice cup of tea?"

"Oh I'd love to, but I don't tend to hang out with dead people. No offence."

I needn't have worried. There was no Hello coming back towards me.

I passed three rooms on my right, sending a cursory glance into each one. All looked normal except for some objects that looked out of place, even for a place that seemed comfortable being out of time. There was little that was actually modern about the place.

I decided to make my way back to the first room on the right, and as I passed each room on my way back to it, I noticed something that was extremely strange to me.

Each room appeared to be eerily laid out in the same manner.

One would expect a bedroom for guests, a master bedroom, perhaps two or three smaller bedrooms. But each seemed to be exactly the same size in terms of width and length.

There was a window to the far wall, a multi-coloured carpet with a rug on top. A fake – at least I hope it was fake tiger rug, with its mouth wide open and I felt its eyes, once again, locked onto me. It was as if the eyes in the portraits downstairs not only were moving in their pictures, but moving to other inanimate objects in the house.

To the right side of the room was the bed. Another portrait hung above it. God, I did not want to look at the portrait. But I did.

I looked at it. I was less scared upon casting my eyes on the painting because it was not a portrait – it was a landscape of a kind that was familiar to me.

It looked like the grounds behind the school. Looking away from the picture, I saw a wardrobe. It was huge, and my legs felt heavy as I walked towards it. My mind kept telling me that there was something extremely nasty in there, and that something meant to cause me harm.

Something began to creak in the room. I know old houses creak like the bones of an old person, but I did not need to experience that particular feeling right now.

On the table next to the bed, was a music box. It was wooden, and its lid had opened. Inside was the figure of a ballerina. Her outfit had been pink at one time, but was now clotted with something dark.

I breathed in a sickening whiff of that earthen, dead bodied smell once again. My heart literally leapt into my mouth as the toy ballerina began started to spin and music churned from within its casing.

I looked around the room. Its appearance seemed to change as my eyes scanned for the details. The room now seemed designed for a younger person, perhaps pre-school. At any other time, in any other house, I don't believe this would have unnerved me. But I decided that this was the time to leave the room. There was no more to learn here.

Everything suggested that I should just go to the end of the landing, and confront what was ever lying in wait for me in the last room. Once they were inside, the house didn't exactly have a reputation for letting people out.

The only way to unravel the mystery would be to do everything in sequence. In fact, I was basing my entire survival on the premise that there actually was a logic to what was going on. As that room had changed before my very eyes, it had to be showing me some kind of snapshot from history.

I approached the next room, expecting to be more confident, but actually finding myself to be feeling far more nervous, unhinged, and scared.

The next room appeared to be considerably larger, but I knew better than that. It was a trick the house was playing on me. It wanted to demonstrate that it was the master, and I was merely a pawn in the game.

All the same, this did appear to be the master bedroom, where a child's parents would sleep. The décor was less colourful than the preceding room. That much was to be expected.

As in the other room, the layout was almost identical. Almost. Instead of a carpet on the floor, the bedroom was bare save for yet another rug that used to walk on four legs at one time.

How many tigers had the owners enjoyed killing? Even if they never pulled the trigger, such people who bought this stuff were part of the problem.

Something caught my attention on this particular tiger rug – it was missing a tooth, and the gum around the gap was still bloody, as if the tooth removal had been recent.

Impossible, yet very possible.

There was a fluttering at the window. I would have had to bypass the tiger-rug to see what it was. It was certainly too big to be a mere pigeon, and they didn't tend to hover. Whatever was outside the window was hovering.

As I watched, it darted away at speed. I breathed a sigh of relief, and prepared to step over the rug, towards a wardrobe that stood near to the eastern wall.

I hoped I would find some answers there.

But my sense of victory, my very sense of purpose unravelled in the next moment. The hovering, fluttering thing by the window had returned. Actually, the sound of its bulbous body splattering on the window outside was the only sound the house was prepared to make.

That, and the obvious creaks of course.

The next sound was of myself, running from the house once more.

I gasped like a deep-sea diver coming up for air as I reached the threshold once more. I had to pass the body of the winged whatever it was, but I cowardly chose to look the other way, even though I could see a broken body and its bloody entrails in the garden's undergrowth.

As I trudged home, my heart belting out of my chest, I felt as far away as ever to finding out the truth.

Act 3

The Ghost of Normandy Road Part IV: The Third and Final Night

I ***hadn't told a single soul. I had not breathed a word to*** anyone, yet, when I arrived at school at 8:30 on the next Monday morning, the playground was alive with the rumour.

A rumour I was doing all I could to dispel.

"You did. We know you did."

"You must be mistaken," I replied indignantly.

But the direct accusations kept on coming, and not just from the usual suspects that were amongst the boys. Though I have to say, their accusations were simple, just as they were.

"You did You did You did," they would say. One of them pushed me. I pushed back. It would be all too easy for me to fall over, my toes being what they now were.

"Stumpy! Stumpy! Call him Tippy-Toe!"
Ah, the name calling. Weren't they just hilarious?

The girls were not given to childish name calling, but the one girl I spoke to about Rebecca was no less direct.

"You can't hide it. You were seen going into that house again. And people are disappearing. They all think you're involved somehow."

She paused to see how I was processing this information. I was pausing before giving an answer. I was trying to decide if she could be trusted or not.

"You're not involved, are you?" she asked me.

"Not in what they're accusing me of, no." It was an answer more honest than I thought I should have given. Still, I had said it now.

"No-one has been in that house two nights in a row. What business have you got there?"

"The kind of business I don't really want to talk about."

She sighed heavily. She could certainly have given my mum a run for her money in this respect. Meanwhile, the boys name-calling had gotten louder. The girl rescued me from them and grabbed my hand.

She dragged me towards the assembly hall. The boys would be expected to put the school chairs out for assembly, so at this time, the hall was empty. The girl wasted no time.

"Take me with you."

Where? The House? *The* house? No. I could not involve her in this. She was being ridiculous and irrational. There you go – two big words that she might not have known the meaning to, but it described her actions perfectly. There was no way in Hell I would take her. The house and I had business of our own to settle. I couldn't involve anyone else.

"You have *got* to take me. If you don't, people really will think that you are *It*. I can be your alibi."

Alibi? Okay, maybe she did have a larger vocabulary than me. I didn't know what that word meant. I'd look it up when all this was over. I wouldn't have to wait that long for its definition to be revealed. She took positive glee in explaining it to me.

"Alibi. It means someone who can vouch for you. I know no-one has accused you of anything yet, but they will."

What she meant was, no real people had accused me of anything, like adults – rational, sensible adults. The boys would accuse me of things just to take the spotlight off of them, but adults like Miss Oakley didn't count, because the old dear was plain crazy. Still, the girl was convinced that if I didn't take her to the house and have her as my alibi, things would get even more unpleasant for me."

"You will see it Danny – you will see it soon enough."

Maybe this was how it was supposed to be. After the last time, I had accepted that more information needed to be uncovered, but I was so terrified each time I went, that I started to believe I would have the condition that ultimately killed my father when I was just a baby. I did not want to have a heart attack, I really didn't.

"I don't even know your name," I said weakly.

"I'm Sarah-Louise," she replied confidently, extending a small hand towards me for me to shake, which I surprised myself by doing. "I'm not scared of you either, and I don't think you did anything bad."

I admit I was a bit taken aback. I thanked her for her support, and from my dealings with Rebecca I knew that girls liked compliments, so I offered one to her.

"Sarah-Louise," I said simply. "It's a nice name."

She smiled. She was pretty – not as pretty as Rebecca, but there was certainly something appealing about her.

"So can we go tonight?" she asked. "After school?"

My mind started to race with thoughts of Rebecca. I didn't want to upset her. What if she and Sarah-Louise weren't friends? Or what if they were? I didn't want there to be any conflict between any of us.

"When are you *eleven*, Danny?" she asked, with the confidence that she was already older than me. Back then, a few months counted.

"July," I said.

"It's April for me, which means I'm senior to you. So now you definitely have to take me. Here. It'll replace your damaged one."

Sarah-Louise fiddled about with her hair, and after pulling some pins and metal from it, her hair hung loose.

"Is this better?"

It was. I couldn't help but break out into a smile for the first time in ages. I was beginning, somehow, to recover from the loss of Rebecca. I just thought she would have stayed in contact, even though this was our last year at primary school.

The object she gave me was a hairpin, much longer than Rebecca's, and I felt ashamed to say, much better quality.

It was quite heavy, looked to be gold plated, and had a long pin that ran alongside the clasp. This was heavy duty.

"Is this an antique or something?"

"Actually it is. It belonged to my great-great grandmother, if you can believe that."

"I can't take this from you, Sarah-Louise."

"You took it from *her*, didn't you? So you can take this from me. Be careful with it though, it's very sharp."

"I don't know where she is now," I said weakly.

"Oh I don't know about that....I really think you do," Sarah-Louise replied cryptically. "Because no-one of any right mind would enter that house on their own."

"Maybe they'll demolish it," I spoke with hope rather than confidence.

"No, they won't," said Sarah-Louise. "That sort of thing costs money. In any case, it will stay standing until it gives up its secrets. The human body works just the same."

Perhaps she knew more than she was letting on. There was no time to debate things further, as the school bell rang for us to prepare to go to assembly. I was shocked as

Sarah-Louise planted a kiss on my cheek and told me she'd see me later.

* * *

The assembly hall was full. But there were some very notable exceptions. There was no Miss McManus. No Miss Oakley. No sign of the boy who had stolen Rebecca's tooth – the one who had his throat cut in the window; an act that I definitely saw happen. Of course it happened. Why else would everyone in that house be wearing black, unless they were going to his funeral? And I never thought to ask the man just how he got that envelope and knew how to give it to me. My mind felt just that little bit too small for the task.

As the children filed quietly into their seats, there was some discussion, some gasps, some words spoken louder than others, resulting in the teachers on the stage hushing us abruptly.

A number of boys were behind me, whilst I was looking for Sarah-Louise. She was three rows back, and I felt relieved to know she was safe. One boy dug a finger into my ribs, referring to the day I saw the girl dragging the human head.

"I don't want some loon sitting next to me," he said.

"Funny. That's just what I was thinking," I retorted.

That shut him up, but what shut us both up was the glare from the head teacher. We were all expecting them to say something about Miss McManus - Miss Oakley, even.

We sang hymns, said prayers, and that...that was it. Oh, there was a mention about Miss Oakley going on something called *gardening leave*. I had no idea what that was, but I could have guessed that Sarah-Louise would know.

Something she said kept running through my head, about 'No-one in their right mind would enter that house on their own.' It sounded to me like a rather inflammatory thing to say. Sarah-Louise was pretty enough, but she was no Rebecca. I missed her so much.

Maybe it was something or nothing. Sarah-Louise had inferred that she did want to go with me to the house, and I felt I could use her support.

So after assembly, and just before class, I decided I would ask her.

Assembly ended without any drama. Sarah-Louise was chatting with two other girls, and I was about to run up to her when a firm arm grabbed me, and threw me against the wall.

There was a door marked PRIVATE which the figure, a boy in my year, but much stronger than me – clearly, pushed me into. Rebecca had always told me those doors were locked. This boy must have had some kind of inside information, because the door opened with ease.

"I won't have you talking to Sarah-Louise. She doesn't like you, get it? Anyone around you ends up in a bad way, and I won't let that happen to her."

His forearm was across my chest. I could scarcely breathe with the pressure.

"I'm not to blame," I screeched. "I don't know what happened."

"Miss Oakley slapped you, but I'll break your neck if you go anywhere near Sarah-Louise. Now you've been warned."

He could have been an ex-boyfriend, a future boyfriend or even her brother. Or just some freak who stalked her. I had no idea. But suddenly, the pressure was off my chest and he stormed out of the room, which shouldn't have been marked PRIVATE at all. It was only filled with filing cabinets, plastic buckets, and a couple of upright standing industrial vacuum cleaners.

Above, three shelves up, there was a box filled with old newspapers. One of them had poked out of the box, perhaps on purpose, and whilst I could not see the headline, I could make out a photo. I knew the house, without being able to see the whole image.

It was that blasted house.

I knew I just had to get a hold of that newspaper, but the very item I needed to reach it – like a stepladder, was nowhere to be seen.

Standing on my tip-toes, even back when I had full use of them, would not have made me close enough to reach the newspaper.

I looked around in the near-dark for a light switch, and was relieved to have found one. The room became bathed in light, and yet seemed like no-one had been inside it for years. Cobwebs laced the shelves and each corner of the room. The filing cabinets wheezed from having far too many documents to hold.

I knew it was not going to be easy, and if I wanted to get that newspaper, I would have to make a mess. I just didn't want to get caught making a noise.

Looking above me, there was nothing for it, except to go for it. I punched upwards, hitting the underside of the box. It fell to the floor with an almighty crash, but whilst I covered my mouth from the dust, I attempted to find a place to hide.

A few moments passed, then a few more, and yet no-one had tried the door. I kept my eyes trained on the door handle, but it did not turn. Everyone, pupil and teacher alike passed by the door and even though it was not fully closed, it was lucky for me that no-one decided to let their curiosity get the better of them.

I unfolded the newspaper, a *Birmingham Post* that was dated some twenty years before I was born. It was a picture of Number 110, Normandy Road, bearing the headline HOUSE OF EVIL FINALLY DEMOLISHED.

What? Demolished?

There was a lot of text around the picture, plus a News Special in the inside pages. The editorial read like this:-

'Scene of many an unexplained murder, the only fully detached house on Normandy Road was finally demolished today, much to the pleasure of local residents. One of them who lived in the house opposite the red-brick coloured building stated that they were glad to see the house go,

retelling a story about their son who committed suicide after being taunted by a demon said to exist in that very house.

Of course, this newspaper can only report the story as we are told. There is no evidence to substantiate this story.'

Oh, but the paper was wrong. There was an overwhelming body of evidence to back the story up. I tried to make sense of it in my head. The story either referred to the boy I knew across the road – the one and same boy who stole Rebecca's tooth, or someone else.

That meant that this horrible death had happened to someone before, and would happen again. With great reluctance and an agonising sense of dread, I turned over the page.

'The house continued to stand, despite a fire ravaging the building in 1887, a German bomb obliterating the kitchen and servants quarters in 1943 and several apparently unconnected suicides, which ultimately caused the plethora of complaints, insisting that the building should be razed to the ground.'

There were more pictures on the page.

One was of the boy who had originally been sent to the 'special school.' It was an old-style photograph which didn't look like it had been taken with any modern photographic equipment.

Even the school clothes the boy wore did not look like the current school uniform we had, but there was one link at least. His tie was the same as the current school colours. The design, emblem and Latin inscription all matched.

Another photo, and again, I recognised the woman, though she appeared to be wearing clothes that my grandmother would not have looked out of place in.

'Miss Oakley was a well-respected teacher in the community, until the untimely death of her son made her go insane. She had been found by neighbours, repeatedly hitting her son, who claimed to have been at 110 Normandy Road earlier that day. When he refused to come out of a trance, Miss Oakley said in her defence that she had been trying to slap him out of it. Neighbours had another viewpoint, and said she was repeatedly hitting her son, even though he was already dead.'

I shook my head in disbelief. Miss Oakley? *Our* Miss Oakley? How could this be? I looked around me, could see footsteps outside. And then incessant banging started on the door. My racing heart matched its loudness.

Please don't come in. Please.

I clasped my hands together and prayed. I don't think I have ever prayed before, not truly, not really. Not with any reverence. But I did now. God I did.

Please make them go away. Please God, please.

The footsteps making the shadow outside the door loitered a while longer, before finally departing.

I breathed a sigh of relief and looked at the paper once more.

'Rosemary Delaney was said to have been so distraught at not winning the house at auction that she was found hanging from a tree in the woods at Hill Top Green. At first it was thought to have been suicide, but clumps of skin were found under her fingernails. DNA tests revealed that the one who had attacked her was related to her. Even though police found the whole idea improbable, the evidence was conclusive. Mrs Delaney had been strung up on the tree by her daughter Rebecca.'

What? I could not believe what I was reading. No way – there was no way on Earth that this could be true. Meanwhile, a shadow emerged outside the door again, and this time, I was caught out.

There was nowhere to hide.

As the deputy head stood in the doorway, surveying the damage, he appeared to look right through me. The effect of his glare, coupled with being found where I was not supposed to be, caused me to relax and feel wet, though it wasn't as gross as I thought it would be.

"Damned kids turning the place over!" he shouted. "Wait right there and I'll be back."

He wasn't looking at me, not directly, so I wasn't certain who he was talking to, but who cares? I took my chance to run out of the place, taking the paper with me.

Everything looked so strange. I passed the classroom by Sarah-Louise, and she sat on her own, drawing a picture. I could see it – it was a picture of a boy, a boy who looked just like me.

I then scratched the idea of it actually being me. Anyone with brown hair and blue eyes was ten a penny these days. I had some fine notions about myself to think that this girl would actually hold me to her heart so dearly.

A teacher passed by the classroom as I looked in, but she said nothing. She was a supply teacher who had seemingly replaced Miss McManus, and didn't know me to look at.

I chose to say nothing to her either. I wanted Sarah-Louise to look up, but she kept on drawing. The teacher, Mr Flanagan asked her was she finished, and she nodded to confirm that she was.

"What an interesting drawing. A boy holding a hair pin. Is this someone special to you, Sarah-Louise?"

It was meant as a playful joke, but Sarah-Louise looked at Mr Flanagan so strangely. Then she turned to the door, looked directly at me, and screamed loud enough to wake the dead from the nearby cemetery.

The scream was blood-curdling – there was no other way to describe it.

Tears streamed down my face, and I rolled the newspaper up, for fear of getting it wet. I would have to read it later. I ran home, but when I arrived there, a FOR SALE sign was up outside.

I knocked on the door and screamed for my mother, but she was nowhere to be found.

People were on the road, but took no notice of me.

It was then, that I saw her.

"Hi Danny. You look a bit lost."

With her golden ginger hair, pretty floral dress and cheeky, impish smile, Rebecca made everything alright again.

"Rebecca. Oh my God. Am I glad to see you. Everything's going crazy. Where have you been?"

"I'm sorry, Danny, I had some things to attend to. But it's okay, I'm not leaving you now."

"I can't find my mother. It says the house is up for sale."

"Yes, that happened to me too. After the *incident*."

"What incident?"

"Don't be so coy, Danny. You have the answer in your own hands."

Rebecca pointed to the newspaper.

"It says the house had been demolished."

"Now didn't your mother ever tell you not to believe all you read in the newspapers?"

Actually, my mother had never said that.

"Rebecca, none of this is making sense."

"Come with me," she said.

I followed Rebecca, who slowed down to my pace. She linked her fingers with mine, and we made our way down Normandy Road. I had forgotten all about Sarah-Louise. I was with Rebecca, and that was all that mattered.

We approached the red-brick house, which according to the newspaper in my arms should not be standing. I passed it alongside Rebecca, who finally stopped outside number 116, just three doors away.

"Why are we stopping here? This was the house you were supposed to be moving into."

Rebecca did that weird pointing of her finger again, away into the distance, but in the direction of the house.

"Can you see inside the living room?" she asked me.

"Of course I can," I said, straining my neck. "There's your father."

"So it is, with his new woman," she said. "She would have been my step-mother."

I wanted to ask her what happened to her mother, but I knew, and Rebecca knew that I knew.

"They live here," she said, "but we live there." Again, Rebecca pointed, only this time, towards the big red-brick house.

It had changed. It had been done up. Perhaps there had been a new auction. Her hand clasped around mine once more, and she walked me in the direction of the house.

"Rebecca…" I began.

"Don't be scared," she said. "You've been here before. There's really nothing to be scared of."

We crossed into the garden, which was full of flowers, and a well-kept green. No wild overgrowth here. The door was magnificent in its finery; constructed of thick oak panels with a small window near its head.

Rebecca lightly touched the door and it swung back gracefully. Inside, the splendour of the hall was mesmerising. In place of strange portraits where the subject's eyes followed you around the room, was one of a building to my left, and a landscape to my right.

Both were familiar to me, yet I could not quite place them, at least I could not yet identify them. She led me up the stairs, and we stopped outside the room on the right. The one which had the music box with the ballerina in. Music clinked from it, and I looked inside the room. It looked different to the other day when I had last visited it. Now it looked clean, fresh and lived-in.

"This is my room," said Rebecca happily, "though I want you to visit me whenever you would like."

I stared at her, trying to comprehend the pieces of the puzzle she had just thrown at me. There was no time to process this first room, for I felt myself being dragged towards the next.

"This is the master bedroom. He stays here. I don't like to disturb him. When I do, there's usually a price to pay."

"What do you mean, Rebecca? Tell me!"

"You already know," she replied. "But I'm happy if you got my tooth back. You did, didn't you?"

Finally, some sense amongst the madness.

"Yes, yes I did." I was almost beside myself with joy at the thought of making Rebecca happy.

"So put it *back*."

I rummaged in my pockets for the envelope. I removed the tooth from its package, and it had become grubby, unclean and unsanitary again.

"I don't think I can, Rebecca. Not like this."

"You can, you and you will. Put it in your mouth, then kiss me."

I could see from her expression that she meant every word. I opened my mouth and placed her tooth on my tongue, fully planning to kiss her. Within an instant, she had clasped her mouth to mine, and those moments of extreme happiness came flooding back to me.

"That's better," she said. "Holes aren't good. Never good."

She grinned at me, full beam. Her tooth was now ivory-white, like the rest of them. I shrugged, trying to hide my complete surprise.

"Rebecca, what do you mean, *we stay here*? Who is in there?"

"Oh, don't mind him. He's nasty. Annoying. I don't like him. He makes me do things. Very bad things. Let me show you the next room."

It shouldn't have shocked me to see a familiar sight in the next room, but it did. From the carpet on the floor to the wallpaper that decorated the room, this was, for all intents and purposes, the very same room I had slept in for the last eight years or so. I don't remember our previous home of course.

"Impressive."

"It's how you really want it to be, so it *is*," said Rebecca. "Now come back to my room and I'll show you the rest."

My room. Her room. His room. But this was not my home. Where was my mother? Where was she?

"Open that newspaper of yours, Danny," Rebecca said gently.

'A Halloween prank that seemed innocent at first turned into something much more sinister when a local boy turned a macabre idea into fantasy.

Playing on the legend of the Tooth Fairy, an ethereal but kindly figure that has been the stuff of children's imagination for years, he decided to make a Tooth Fairy suit. His outfit caused outrage and shock to teachers and parents alike, when he turned up on the night of Halloween to trick or treat. He was reported as only being interested in the trick part of the age-old ritual.

He attacked several children, hitting them in the face with a set of pliers, before yanking teeth from them, terrified and scared as they were, yet unable to do anything to fight back.

When asked why he was doing this, he said simply that his name was Seta.

Local children, however, described him as The Tooth Fairy with Blood-Red Wings.'

"That demon is in this house?" I cried. "That's what has been hiding here, all this time."

Rebecca didn't have to answer, because the figure that stood in the doorway resembled the picture of the boy, but was in the body of a man I knew.

The Locum.

"You!" I shouted. "I knew it! I knew there was something wrong with you!"

"Really Danny, sticks and stones.....you know the rest of the saying, don't you?"

"Rebecca! How can you stay with this *thing*? We are leaving, now!"

I tried to sound commanding, but Rebecca stayed put on her bed.

"We're not going anywhere, Danny," she said, "and neither are you. We've got to stay here. This is the base from which we do our work. How else is anyone supposed to believe in us, if we just fade away?"

Then it hit me. No-one knew what I was on about whenever I asked had they seen Rebecca. I took a deep breath before saying the words I never thought I would say. I found myself pointing at the girl I loved.

"You're the Witch of Hill-Top Green."

She smiled. She was the prettiest witch I had ever seen. Not at all like the boys and girls at school had described.

"Yes I am."

"You killed your mother."

"Because she was having an affair with another man, and because she was abusing me. Yes, I killed her."

I turned around to face The Locum, Seta...whatever his name was.

"And you – you're the Tooth Fairy with Blood Red Wings."

He pressed his scaly hands together, and took a bow. Rebecca stood up and took her place next to him. They both extended their hands to me. I had but one question. I suspected the answer was in that newspaper, but I asked them anyway – I asked them who *I* was.

"Oh Danny, you already know," giggled Rebecca.

"You're *the Ghost of Normandy Road*."

Epilogue

I opened the newspaper, and it told me all that I didn't want to know.

'Many years have passed since the first sighting of the infamous Ghost of Normandy Road. Some say the sightings became more frequent over the dark winter months, but in a recent and disturbing event, the malevolent spirit is believed to have infiltrated the local school.

One of the students, eleven-year old Sarah-Louise Duffy confirmed to this newspaper that she had seen the spirit a number of times.

"I even spoke to it," she said. "I gave him a keepsake of mine – a hairpin. A symbol of his long-lost love. I hoped that if I did that, he wouldn't hurt me."

The long-lost love Miss Duffy speaks of is the girl the Ghost fell in love with, before she revealed what her true nature was. A monster completely bereft of kindness, and utterly incapable of love.

And the name of this 'monster'? It had been heard in the school hall, the girls' toilets and in various other locations around the school – the name of this particular girl was Rebecca.

Local historians believe this entity to be the ghost of Rebecca Delaney, but given her possession by the demon known as Seta – something which is the subject of much disrepute amongst scholars, this publication cannot be certain.

What is for certain is that the young girl fought with her mother when Mrs Delaney's alcohol and drug fueled moods reached a new low point. Tired of the physical, emotional and mental torture, which had escalated into sexual abuse, in the end, it is believed that the young girl found some supernatural strength within her to subdue her mother. Or maybe she had help. Their bodies were found in the woods beyond Hill Top Green.

She cursed her mother, who, far from being repentant and acknowledging her actions, chose to curse her back. As the rope was secured around Mrs Delaney's neck, she screamed that Rebecca would never leave the woods alive, that any beauty she had would be taken from her. In addition, when human eyes were fixed upon her, they would only see evil, ugliness and hatred.

Mrs Delaney probably did not believe that Rebecca never intended to leave the woods alive. She planned to kill herself all along – anything to end the torture.

I raised my eyes up from the newspaper, my hands shaking, that is to say if what I held the document with could be termed as being hands. They looked so strange to me, my digits were missing their fingernails. The skin was taut and pale. I could see veins through the back of my hands. What was happening to me? I had every right to view Rebecca as a monster, but all I could see was a girl who looked completely beautiful to my eyes.

Beautiful, tortured, dead Rebecca. The love of my life was *dead*. I was realising this and much more besides. Still, I had to question everything, and even when the evidence pointed to the obvious, I could not accept it.

"But I was at the school, Rebecca. You were my girlfriend, weren't you? We kissed, didn't we? You gave me your hairpin, didn't you? Miss McManus, Miss Oakley, Mr Flanagan. They all spoke to us. They interacted with us. Are you saying all of that wasn't real? That it was all in my mind? Images jumbled together of a past life, or many past lives?"

She smiled at me. There was *some* love there, but it was tinged with sadness. Sadness because of what she had become. Not my love anymore, but a monster, a demon, a *devil*. This was what Rebecca truly was. I could not hate her for it. Rather the opposite, actually. I pitied her.

But I had no recollection of what I had done or the evil acts I was recorded as committing. Why would I do that? I was good boy, wasn't I?

"No, Danny, you're not wrong, it was real enough. But there had to be some way to get you to me. I was jealous of that first girl you liked, that Sarah-Louise. The girl you read about in the paper. Do you remember how you used to feel about her? Well, I didn't like that. I didn't like that at all. I did all in my power to stop it. I made her go away, just like I made them all go away. But I really liked you. You were fun for a while. But I had a greater purpose in mind, and I had to find a way to *keep* you."

I could not accept what she was saying. I *loved* this girl. I don't care what anyone says. If we had been adults and split up, those around us would have said *Move on, you will find someone else. Someone better.* But that's not what I wanted. Did this fantasy version of Rebecca exist only in my mind? When she called me her love, her soul mate, her twin flame, were all of those statements lies? A new sensation, a physical one, joined my mental torture and shared a merry macabre dance together. Like a rose opening its petals, a bloody gash materialised between my shoulder blades. I winced with the pain, smoothed my palm over it, and when I looked at my hand, it was covered with blood.

"You *killed* me? I don't believe it. I can't believe you would ever do something like that to me."

Rebecca seemed unconcerned with my statement, which might have sounded like I was challenging her, but I wasn't. I was at my wits end trying to *understand*.

"Seta said that we needed a third one in our group. The Witch of Hill Top Green, that's a legend that has been the very reason kids and adults alike don't journey to the woods beyond Hill Top Green alone. The Tooth Fairy with Blood-Red Wings was another play on what really scared children. As for you, Danny…well, you were a lot more difficult. Your body didn't want to rest. We had a lot of problems with you. Seta didn't even want you to have a proper burial, but, I don't know…out of some kind of care for you, I insisted. You may not believe it, but I love you more than you think. I am just not that good at showing it. You are far more empathic than me. Your completeness is what completes me. I latch onto that which I desire, and I desired you, Danny. When your body could not find peace, we came up with the idea of a new horrifying legend, which became the Ghost of Normandy Road. The locals…they sure believed it. But if *you* don't believe me now, if you continue to refuse to accept what has really happened to you *and* the gravity of what you have done since, then….we will have to repeat this whole cycle all over again."

I was taking all of this in, when she pressed me for an answer. As if *answers* mattered now.

"What am I supposed to do?"

I hated how I sounded. Weak in death as well as in life? What had been the point of me, young Danny, ever existing?

Rebecca spoke with confidence and in matter of fact manner well beyond her ten years. But of course, she was not ten years old. She wasn't even a human girl, and had not been one for a very long time. Time no longer meant anything to me. What was going to have any meaning now? If I didn't know, Rebecca – *the Witch*, was certain to tell me.

"You can start by bringing others to us. Someone familiar, someone you know. How about Sarah-Louise? Bring her to us. In fact, bring her to *me*. I have some things I would like to do to Sarah-Louise."

What in the world was happening? Whatever Rebecca had in mind for Sarah-Louise, it sounded anything but pleasant. My love for Rebecca…crystal-clear for me in the past, was anything but clear now. I loved her, but I also *didn't* love her. I didn't want her to hurt Sarah-Louise. I didn't want her to hurt anybody.

I walked past Rebecca to peer out of the window of the big old house. I could now see the world from a totally new perspective. My work, if you could call it that, would begin the very next day.

I felt an ice-cold hand touch my back. Deep and twisted between my shoulder blades lay a permanent memory – a constant reminder of precisely where she stabbed me. In that moment, I was fully seized of what she felt for me – love, hatred, jealousy, vengeance. But more than anything, I felt her sense of unending love. It was twisted, hardly a fairytale, but it was love nonetheless.

We would never leave the house on Normandy Road. *This* was our existence now. We would go out sometimes, but the idea, as Rebecca had stated, was to bring things, people and events to *us*. I'd like to think that I had a choice in the matter, but she had made it for me. That's how I knew I could exist for ten thousand lifetimes and not know for sure if she ever truly loved me. Then, she did something that made me believe she knew what I was thinking.

Rebecca moved her hand and wrapped an arm around my waist. Suddenly, I felt her love for me again. It was confused, warped and not love in the truest sense. But it was the best that she could give to me.

Rebecca rested her head on my shoulder and joined me in looking out at our twisted new world. She'd never say *I love you, Danny* because she was incapable of doing so. In the past, when I was *convinced* we were meant for each other, she would show her love in different ways, because the way we communicated our affection was often at odds with how I would have really liked it to be.

Still, she was here with me now and I was with her. Our twisted union would continue, but in a way I had never envisaged. But maybe we've done these ten thousand times already. I had to accept the situation for now, so I did. I was happy with Rebecca. I wanted to tell her, but she said something to me first.

"*Darling*," she said.

The Real Normandy Road: *A History*

Birmingham, England. 1981.

Normandy Road isn't exactly the prettiest of roads, but it was an essential one to navigate if I wanted to get to my junior school, the Roman Catholic 'Sacred Heart'.

I passed the red-bricked house on Normandy Road every day on the walk back from school. Sometimes I would be with my mum, other times I would be walking back with my sister, who was two years older than me.

I could recall running down Normandy Road with my sister, in the snowy landscape of Christmas 1980 and the following January in 1981. We were both small then, and the snow patterns were more regular in the UK in those days. As kids, we knew nothing about the climate change or the O-Zone layer. We were just children, being children.

Everything would have looked huge to us, I suppose, but that house stood out then, and still stands out, though much less imposing to me as it once was.

So why did I decide to write about it? Well, my thoughts processes were hampered by what kind of book it should be. Should I write a work of non-fiction – one where it was about the dry details of a haunted house and my recollections of it? This may have been the easier task. Any fiction writer would probably agree that creating a work of pure fantasy is much harder. It must be *believable*, the characters must be ones you can relate to, and of course, the plot must flow and remain coherent throughout.

At school, it was quite to discover all sorts of things that would frighten us, and as I have aged, I promised myself that I would never lose touch with my inner child, and with it, my sense of wonder and curiosity about life. There are so many things out there in the world that are free, yet we let ourselves get too busy with work, or worry about things that we cannot possibly control. I am as guilty of this behaviour as the next person. It does not stop me trying from aiming to do better.

Like all books I write, and I expect many writers are the same; a story begins with ideas and notes, many of which can come when one is at their most relaxed. As I tend to write quite intense stories, I am not lost on the irony of this.

The *Rebecca* of this story was a real girl, a real person, and obviously we both had great fun whilst at school. I was utterly devastated to know she had moved on, and I did not know where she had gone to.

These days, you can find people from yesteryear quite easily using social media, so Facebook and Twitter et al have their uses in this regard. I've also been incredibly blessed that people from that school did contact me, and I have rekindled a thirty-year-old friendship with them.

On recent trips back to the road itself, I don't feel scared at all. Maybe it's because I'm much older now, and what scared me as a child would not do so now.

The photo I took is of the actual house, taken in 2016. Of course, it's a good thing that old houses are maintained, but comparisons with my memory of it as a child, to how it stands today, vary to such a degree, it is hard to believe it is the same house.

It has maintained its red-brick design, but of course, red brickwork is common to many Birmingham houses, indeed Midlands wide. I believe this is because much of the brickwork can herald its formation back to Ironbridge in Shropshire, thus being responsible for the colours on our house bricks today.

Is this deliberate? When I visited the house for real as a child, it would have been easy to say that the bricks were so-coloured because *blood* was that colour.

The renovated house on Normandy Road, picture taken in 2016

It's also fair to say that I was rather squeamish as a child. I did not care for the sight of blood at all, would avoid any talk about it or any programmes about hospitals.

So why did I become largely known as a writer of horror fiction? All I can tell you is that I never liked any particular situation or condition to get the better of me. That is not to say I want to become a neurologist at some point in the future. Let us just say that for the most part, I have conquered a good many demons in my life.

It's been a long while since I first entered that house. Do we do what we are told as children? I'm sure we do, for the most part. But a parent, teacher, indeed any adult in authority would not want to kill the curiosity monster inside us, surely? Our need to explore, to have an adventure, even one laced with some element of danger, should remain appealing to us, for all of our lives. As I age, I don't want to get too comfortable. We have to push ourselves out of that comfort zone sometimes, lest we find ourselves pushed.

In my case, my actions were all my own. There were no dares sent my way from other boys or girls. I just wanted to know the story behind that particular house. I wanted to know why it stood on its own, with no-one to seemingly care about it.

This is what I remember.

The smart thing to do would have been to try and enter the house on a Spring or Summer's Day. I was very introverted as a child, and activities like this looked great on television, with kids getting up to all sorts of things, but for me, I was a passive observer. It was far better not to take part in such things. I played it safe. Maybe that's a good thing, because I'm still here today.

As for any regrets about what I haven't done in my life, and especially during a time when I had no responsibilities at all, I don't waste my time on such negative thoughts, as we certainly can't be born again.

The house was intriguing to me, that's the only way to put it.

Perhaps it was the sheer size of the place that was most impressive to me at first. I wondered how such a big house could be left to rot. Its many windows were cracked, and some had been broken, I would guess – by a football, a stone or a brick.

The brickwork itself was in good condition. The roof looked okay for the most part, but as I would find out later, it had sustained some wear and tear. Because of the lack of proper maintenance, there were several damp areas in the house.

I didn't have a bicycle back then. As in the fictional story, I believe I was around eight years old when I first went into the house. Two years earlier, I had possessed a tricycle, and I lost control of it when riding too fast down an underpass (U.S. – *subway*) and damaged my right knee, when I managed to collide with a wall.

I would not own a bicycle again until my early teens, so where-ever I went, it was on foot or travel by bus.

As I passed the house every day from school anyway, it was not a far distance to walk. I cannot really tell you what possessed me to finally go into the place. Perhaps it was a rites of passage kind of thing, a belief that I wouldn't be able to grow as a person if I didn't actually try and test myself.

This was a big challenge for someone rather introverted.

Although the fictional story you have just read clocked up a decent amount of positive reviews since its release in the summer of 2015, and collected a silver award for its category (Young Adult Horror) by *Readers' Favourite*, it could have been this factual element that you could have ended up reading instead.

It is true that the fictional story was indeed a work of fiction, but there were some things about it that were absolutely true. So for a short while, I was in two minds as to whether I should write a book that was pure non-fiction, or craft a work of fiction. In the end, the creative side of my brain made that decision for me.

Whilst some readers will have found 'Ghost' a bit too scary for young readers, I have to admit that if I picked this book up, aged around ten or twelve, it would have been precisely the kind of book I would have loved to have had the opportunity to read. On the book's product page, it states that *everyone loves a good ghost story*. I think that is true, because even people who don't like horror stories or movies take this position precisely because it is successful in its aim – to scare, in much the same way as a comedy will hopefully cause people to laugh, or a romance to cause people to love being in love.

I have had people of all ages read the book, and many of them said it scared them out of their wits. Others focussed on other elements, how it is a tale of a first love as much as anything else.

I changed the names of the main characters as I did not wish to reveal the true name of the girl in question who was the first girl I was really attracted to. In the story, that girl is named Rebecca, and I chose the name of Danny in part because of the character in the Stephen King horror *The Shining*, and I wanted to pay homage to that book.

My mother and I would often watch movies to see in the new year when we were younger, and I would typically pick a horror movie to bridge the gap between the old year and the new one. We were not ones for singing Auld Lang Syne. We wanted to view something really spectacular, and after the first thirty seconds of watching them erupt in the sky or on television, we concluded that not only were fireworks rather boring, they were pretty irritating. There's something to be said for not being famous or in positions of power. If I was the monarch, prime minister or a Z-list celebrity, I would have to attend one of those ghoulish ceremonies to see the new year in. That was my idea of Hell. These days, if I can't see in the new year with the one I love, I head to bed early. Come to think of it, if I was with the one I love, we'd be heading to bed early in any case.

Most horror writers will have been inspired to write by one author or another, perhaps several. In my early teens, I would head out to Birmingham city centre via the 33 or 51 bus, and go direct to WH Smith, Dillons or Waterstones to view the latest best sellers. I could not have known that in the future, I too would an author, looking for my books amongst those same authors that first inspired me. Currently, as I publish direct, my titles are not seen in WH Smith's bookstores alongside Stephen King, Dean R Koontz or Anne Rice, but that doesn't mean that one day, they won't be. I actually do believe they could take their place alongside such notable literary masters. But I don't kid myself. Even though it seems like I have been writing for decades, the hard writing phase for me probably began in 2011. Compared to those authors listed above, it is a case of small beans. I have much to live up to.

My late teen / early twenties forays into writing went from bizarre – *Nuclear B*stards*, a tale about a group of misfits who went from galaxy to galaxy righting wrongs, to *2089* – Two Thousand and Eighty-Nine a futuristic science fiction yarn about a female cyborg that was aiming to develop her own personality and life journey, much to the chagrin of her owners. Lastly, around 2002-3 I had penned a violent thriller called *The Seventh Siste*r, about a young girl who was the only survivor of a brutal slaughter of her entire family, and how she set out to take revenge on the perpetrators.

None of those stories would have been good enough to publish directly or traditionally, but we do improve the more we work at anything we set our mind to. Of those three story drafts, The Seventh Sister is probably the only one I could make workable enough to publish. In any case, the truth is, you don't know what you have written until someone tells you what you've done. You can have a view, you can have a clear purpose for the book you create. The writer, I believe, does have a responsibility to their audience. If they have a fanbase, those readers will come to expect a certain kind of book from you, and they will quite rightfully demand a high standard. The readers who you haven't found yet, as an author, will scrutinise your works far harder than the first group. That doesn't mean you stop working hard. Each word, sentence and paragraph had better make sense, otherwise some reviews may be rather harsh.

As an author, I have developed a rather thick skin. Some people have a skin so thick that not only are they impervious to criticism, they downright believe that criticism is below them. I actually believe some criticism is helpful, but the author knows whether or not he has given the world his best. That is all I have ever aimed to do.

With *The Ghost of Normandy Road* being a 2015 release, some years have passed already. I was happy with it at the time, but wanted to pen even scarier stories that were entirely from my own mind and not necessarily based on what I experienced as a young schoolboy, walking home by Normandy Road. To some degree, I think the later books, loosely and collectively known as the Normandy Horror Trilogy (*The Ghost of Normandy Road, The Girl Who Collected Butterflies*, and *Children of the Dark Light*) are better than the first story, but that should always be a creator's aim – your most current work should be your favourite one. The singer K.D. Lang was once interviewed and asked that very same question – "Of all your works, which one is your favourite?" and she replied "The newest one."

My most popular books could have more reviews than others I personally feel are amongst my best. There are all sorts of reasons for this. One of my books is free to download if you have a e-reader device. Another was promoted hard on blog tours, when they were popular back in 2014-5. Another is one I promoted the most on sites like ENT, BookSends and others.

This book, however, needed a decent epilogue that would tell you something about me – the writer, and how I shaped those formative experiences into the fiction work that preceded it. I could have rushed it, posted a one-page epilogue and left it at that. These days, the more you publish, the more you are rewarded by the algorithms, but I only publish when I feel the book is ready. I don't think it is a bad idea to publish so frequently, but I personally want my story to breath, the plot to develop, the characters to grow. I, for one, could not do that if I published every month.

I think the best stories, especially those that sit in the horror genre – bring you along with the characters. Not every scene has to build up to a jumpy scare, not every interaction with a demon or monster has to be a bloody event with over the top gore.

In my view, it's the stories that show the frailties and strengths of each character that make you care for them. In the respect of Danny, he knew that Rebecca was his love – everything happened to be mere circumstance. Whether you decide Danny, Rebecca, or indeed, the ominous house on Normandy Road are evil, or completely innocent, I think it is this element that is the strongest of all. I'm not suggesting for a minute that this book should be relocated in the romance section, but you get what I mean.

The house I focussed on in the story was Number 110, but I also mention Number 116. As a child, I should have paid more attention to the details. For instance, I knew the girl in question lived on Normandy Road, but I was unsure where, even though we had walked down there together a number of times.

When she disappeared in the story, she had also disappeared in my real life. One day, she was there at school, and then, she was gone. The teachers told me that she had moved onto another school at the request of her parents, but there was no way to contact her, no forwarding address, nothing. Isn't it strange that such a brief contact with someone could still impact me decades later? We could not have hung out together for more than one year, but it was a significant year, that much is for certain.

Where would she be now? As there are no other books that I know of about Normandy Road, I wonder what her thoughts would be, not only as someone who had been on that actual road, but as a reader too?

The residents of Normandy Road probably wouldn't thank me for making their habitat well known as a scary place, but as anyone will tell you who has lived long enough, there are scarier things than ghosts, demons or the terrors that tease us on occasion. It's more appropriate to say that people you interact with may be the scariest and most total manifestation of horror that you will ever experience. How many times have you said 'it's a nightmare.' But nightmares are supposed to be something we experience at night, hence the word *night* mare.

My mother often used this phrase, and yes, I could agree that at times, the situation at hand was troubling, difficult, perhaps even horrific, but a nightmare? No, not so much.

The house, number One Hundred and Ten was a ruin back in the 1980s. It was fertile ground for teenagers, young boys like myself, and perhaps more worryingly – squatters, tramps, thieves, hardened drug users and so on.

You would be forgiven for thinking *and this is the place he based the story on?* Well, here's the thing – the house *was* a ruin, and empty – so far as actual humans were concerned. But as I wrote in the foreword to this book, it's that sense of fear that manifests itself in our minds. The reality was that no-one was staying in it. Maybe someone had tried to squat there and ran into the *real* Ghost of Normandy Road.

Oh yes, the ghost exists. Of that, I am in no doubt. True, I was between eight and ten years old when I first went into the house. It's also true how I described the house. The pale red-brick design, the overgrown bushes, the broken front door which had a huge knocker on it, but it was broken and ready to fall to the ground. The imposing windows that functioned like eyes, peering down at those foolhardy enough to cross the threshold.

In the fourth book in the Haunted Minds series, there is an ominous scene where one character crosses the threshold. I built up quite the sense of foreboding in the lead up to that scene, but that's how I felt when first crossing it. So if you felt the fear as one character finally enters the house, you know it is because I actually did it in real life. You had better believe it!

Should authors go to such lengths to make their works of fiction more realistic? I think so. It's not that we are cheating readers if there is something completely out of our hands. For example, I could write a science fiction novel about visiting Mars, but even in my lifetime, such an event may never happen. So as writers, we must tell the truth as far as we can see it. You, the reader, deserve nothing less.

The truth is that a ghost, a presence, some kind of unearthly spectre absolutely resided in Normandy Road. Like some of my characters in other scenes in the Haunted Minds series, I would go to the library, the original Birchfield Library as it was back then, and do my own research. Admittedly, I focussed more on works of fiction rather than non-fiction, but my mother could be trusted to buy me a book that would fire my imagination still further.

I am only in the loosest of contact with one school pupil from all those years ago. She actually read the original Ghost of Normandy Road and enjoyed it, but we haven't really had much to talk about since. I suppose it is because we are very different people from the carefree children we once were at the Sacred Heart School. *People are strange*, so the song goes. When she befriended me online, it was interesting to note that she had maintained friendships with other pupils from that time, whilst I had not. That is not to say I cannot maintain long term friendships. My longest one spans some nineteen years, and in the case of some of my martial arts students, the length is more than two decades.

It is all about making and maintaining connections.

I didn't go into the house on Normandy Road after those first few attempts. It was a scary place. I do wonder if the current owners ever ran into some entity there, be it malevolent or benevolent?

It still commands quite a presence on the road, and stands out more than any other house. There are too many cars on modern-day Normandy Road now, so if it ever becomes famous people will experience some difficulty in going to it. But something tells me the journey will be worth their while.

Also in the Haunted Minds Series

Clara's Song: Haunted Minds II **(2015)**
The Girl Who Collected Butterflies: Haunted Minds III **(2015)**
Children of the Dark Light: Haunted Minds IV **(2017)**
The Seamstress Who Worshipped Beelzebub: Haunted Minds V **(2018)**

The Ghost of Normandy Road

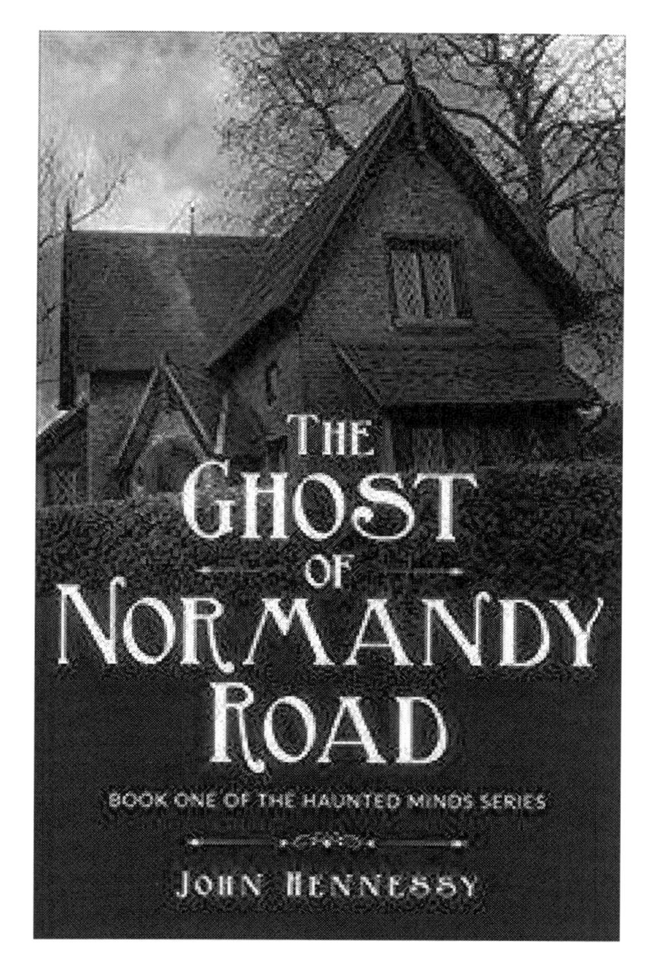

Haunted Minds I

Everyone likes a good ghost story....
...so read this award-winning horror!

The Ghost of Normandy Road (Award Winner (Silver) - Readers Favourite International Book Contest 2016 - YA Horror) : Haunted Minds: I is a riveting haunted house mystery for teens to adults from British Horror fiction author John Hennessy. Especially good for Halloween, it's a dark fairy tale that could be read at any time of year.

Synopsis:-

Three Legends. One True Horror.
An old house stands on Normandy Road, uncared for and uninhabited for years, until one day, believing an urban legend that no-one dares to live there, a young boy decides to cross its threshold.
Yet the house is far from empty - within its walls, a terrible evil has been disturbed.
It will take one brave soul three of the longest nights of his life to unlock its secrets, but will he live to tell the tale?

What other reviewers said.

"The Ghost of Normandy Road has a mature style that left the reader caught in a case of cat & mouse moves. If I was 11 to 13 years of age ... I would be frightened to death. "

- Editorial Review - D.R. Mitton

"Great book for fans of young adult horror and dark fairy tales. I loved the ending. I never saw that coming, and briefly sat stunned at what I had just read."

- Editorial Review - P Mortimer

"Will leave you with a lingering fear in your mind even after reading the book."

- Editorial Review - Book Stop Corner

Clara's Song

Haunted Minds II

Damaged lives. No-one they can trust. And a battle to stay sane.......all while there's a serial killer on the loose.

Following Book One, the award winning *The Ghost of Normandy Road,* Book Two in the Haunted Minds series is entitled Clara's Song - a gripping psychological horror thriller, and a dark twisted tale perfect for fans of women's psychological fiction. Clara's Song features a new group of characters who fight for their sanity as the events around them threaten to destroy all their hopes.

***

Be careful what you wish for.

Clara Bayliss dreams of escaping her boring marriage. When her car fails to start after a freakish accident, her fantasy has every chance of becoming the reality.

Rescued by the very man she thought had been killed, she takes a ride into the unknown with him, and has no intention of returning home. Her husband isn't pleased about being dumped. Especially when he finds out the news she's been keeping from him.

And then, there's a song, the one that Clara would play whenever she needed freeing from a world full of despair.

Clara's Song.

It would make her feel good. Strong. Independent. Fearless.
Only, her rescuer knows the song too, and for him, it means something else entirely.
A dark romance, detective story featuring a seemingly unstoppable serial killer, Clara's Song is psychotic thriller, full of mystery, suspense, lost dreams and total paranoia from which there is no escape.
Mature Content. 18+ only. For fans of contemporary British fiction.

What other reviewers said.

"Must read for all psycho horror lovers. "
Editorial Review - A.S.
"Trust John to make romance so horrifying."
Editorial Review - read / watch / think
"I don't know whether to feel sad, happy, inspired or freaked out. This was a story that took my mind into a complete abyss."

Editorial Review - J.K.

"This is a psych horror that is scary because of how seemingly normal people can lose their mind and even scarier than that, their sense of reality."
Editorial Review - Charlee-babez

"Not many writers dare to write about such things."
Editorial Review – KSN

"Clara's Song is dark and intriguing and it certainly messes with your head. "
Editorial Review - LL.

"The adult nature of the violence and sexual scenes may upset some, I think it will attract more readers than it will repel. A brave book with an engaging storyline and characters to match."
Editorial Review - Caitlin's Book Review

The Girl Who Collected Butterflies

Haunted Minds III

The race is on to stop a killer.

But how can she be stopped?

Boys made fun of her. Girls tended to avoid her. Teachers didn't understand her.
Marissa Coton collected butterflies.

For her Very Special Project, Marissa took some butterflies and placed a name under each one.
To her classmates, the selection appeared to be random. No harm done.
But when the children in Marissa's book begin to die in mysterious circumstances, the evidence points to the mysterious girl with black eyes who wears a red bow in her hair.

There's method in her apparent madness. There's a reason why she's doing it. By the time her secret is out, it will be far too late. Because if someone threatens her, their secrets will be revealed to the world.
The race is on to stop her from killing anyone else, but how can she be stopped?

***

Part of the Haunted Minds series of books, 'The Girl Who Collected Butterflies' is a psychic thriller and unexplained mystery novel - an indirect follow-up to book one, 'The Ghost of Normandy Road.'
Mature content - recommended for 15 years of age and over. Story contains strong swearing, gore and violence, some sexual references.

What other reviewers said.

Editorial Reviews:-

"This is a John Hennessy book in the raw...There is nothing more frightening to me than a creepy child. Regardless of age, they freak me out. Marissa's character was written so very well, I could almost feel her eyes staring at me from the pages.
- J. K.

"We all had projects at school, a Science one or a Geography one. The main character, Marissa has one but hers is one full of evil...or is it, or is she trying to right a wrong?
All the characters have depth to them in fact I think John Hennessy has excelled in this area. The main character and secondary characters are all

engaging, believable and it is up to the reader to like or dislike them. When I met one character I really detested them but as the book progressed my feelings towards that one individual changed...such is the power of description and narrative."
- S.B.

"Sinister and creepy, evil to the core."
- A.S.

Children of the Dark Light

Haunted Minds IV

She's dead. But she's still coming to get you.
Can a paranormal activity buff avoid the wrath of the dead ones?
A beautiful house of dark red brick and gothic style stands on Normandy Road. It has had many inhabitants over the years, and is about to gain some new tenants.

However, the house has never truly been empty. There's something there, and it has always been there. To some, the horrors that reside in Normandy Road are just myths, legends, and in the present day, there is nothing to be scared of.

But there are some that have seen and felt their presence. Their sleep is ripped apart as the nightmarish entities that reside there manage to torment their day.

Something lives in that house. It senses its time has come. A time of evil. Sometimes, they work on their own. Collectively, they are known as The Dead Ones, to others they are known as the Children of the Dark Light; and as improbable and implausible as it may seem; somehow, somewhere, you've met them before

The Seamstress Who Worshipped Beelzebub

Haunted Minds V

She was a lost soul on the ninth of her cats' lives and she knew it. She always had an angle, a way of twisting things, a sob-story for anyone who would listen. One by one, kind words softly spoken from well-wishers fell into silence.

But the voices in her head are far from quiet. They taunt her with rose-tinted views of her past, and terrifying images of her future. Sex, drugs and alcohol blur her every waking moment. She needs saving from herself, because her fixes are killing her.

A woman with an unusual set of skills offers her a chance to reshape her past, live with her present, and create an unknown but possibly happier future.

A chance to save herself from making her Hell on Earth, a Hell for all Eternity.

But just what is the cost of her redemption, and what price is she willing to pay?

***

Part of the award winning Haunted Minds series of books.

--

MATURE CONTENT 18+ Contains adult content. Not to be read by minors / people under the age of 18. Contains sexual content, drugs, religious references and strong scenes of psychological terror that some readers will find disturbing

By the same Author

FICTION

Dark Winter: The Wicca Circle **(2013)**
Stormling (Book One of the Mordana Chronicles) **(2014)**
Dark Winter: Crescent Moon **(2014)**
Murderous Little Darlings: A Tale of Vampires: I **(2014)**
The Blood and the Raven: A Tale of Vampires: II **(2015)**
Innocent While She Sleeps: A Tale of Vampires: III **(2015)**
Dream the Crow's Black Dream: A Tale of Vampires: IV **(2015)**
The Ghost of Normandy Road: Haunted Minds I **(2015)**
Clara's Song: Haunted Minds II **(2015)**
The Girl Who Collected Butterflies: Haunted Minds III **(2015)**
Dark Winter: Last Rites **(2016)**
Reunion of the Blood: A Tale of Vampires: V **(2016)**
The Halloweeners **(2016)**
Dawn of the New Breed: A Tale of Vampires: Prequel **(2016)**
Children of the Dark Light: Haunted Minds IV **(2017)**
11:47 – Small Slices of Horror Vol 1 **(2017)**
Kirsty the Most Powerful Witch in the World **(2017)**
The Halloweeners II **(2017)**
The Seamstress Who Worshipped Beelzebub: Haunted Minds V **(2018)**
Our Hearts Go to Their Graves: A Tale of Vampires: VI **(2020)**
One More Story: A Thriller **(2020)**

COLLECTIONS

Three Tales of Vampires **(2015)**
Dark Winter Trilogy **(2016)**

NON-FICTION

The Essence of Martial Arts **(2011)**
The Essence of Martial Arts: Special Edition **(2013)**
How to Write, Keep Writing and Keep Motivated: Tips for Aspiring Authors **(2015)**
Coco: Joy of After-Life (2018)
The Mastery of Martial Arts: End Fights in Seconds **(2018)**

Forthcoming Releases

FICTION

Murderous Little Darlings 2
The Haunting of Witterwick House
The Halloweeners III

NON-FICTION

The Mastery of Martial Arts: Second Edition
Gui-Gui: The World's Greatest Cat

Finally...

If you enjoyed this book, please consider leaving a review. Visit my website or my Amazon books page. Don't forget to grab Murderous Little Darlings, and make sure you get The Blood and the Raven too for free by signing up to my mailing list. Thank you so much for reading my work.

Keep up to date at JohnHennessyBooks.com

Make sure you visit the official author website for British author John Hennessy. News, updates and giveaways will be posted here.

www.JohnHennessyBooks.com

Printed in Great Britain
by Amazon